THE SECRET CITY

CHRIS ARCHER

SCHOLASTIC INC.
New York Toronto London Auckland Sydney
Mexico City New Delhi Hong Kong Buenos Aires

ISBN 0-439-36851-0

Copyright © 2003 17th Street Productions,
an Alloy, Inc. company
All rights reserved.
Published by Scholastic Inc.

Produced by 17th Street Productions,
an Alloy, Inc. company
151 West 26th Street
New York, NY 10001

12 11 10 9 8 7   3 4 5 6 7 8/0

Printed in the U.S.A.   40
First Scholastic printing, January 2003

The key to good fortune lies in the heart.

Canis Marinus

S.O.

I

W.K.
MDCXCIX

One
THE DARE

"Hey, awesome party, George!"

Shannon Starling walked up to George van Gelder and gave him a little punch on the arm. She ran a hand through her orange-streaked hair and then smiled as she looked around the small backyard, fenced in by an ivy-covered brick wall. It was George's eleventh birthday, and the party his dad had thrown for him was just winding down.

"Thanks, Shannon," George said with a shy smile. "Too bad the Diversions had to cut it short."

Shannon grinned. Her band, the Diversions, had played at the party until the police showed up to investigate noise complaints. But Shannon didn't seem to mind. The Diversions were never happy unless someone complained about them.

Shannon was right; George's party had been a smashing success. The normally sleepy New York backyard had filled with lively guests, and the pile of presents by the back door had grown sky-high.

Now most of the people were gone, and George felt tired but happy. The only guests left in the back garden were Shannon and George's friend Derrick Wilson. The three sat down to relax, looking up at the evening sky.

"I'll make you a tape," Shannon promised.

"You don't have to do that," George said quickly. For his birthday, Shannon had already given him a mix tape full of songs. Thankfully, only one was by the Diversions. Actually, all of George's presents had been pretty good. The Diversions' drummer, Renee Kozinski, had given him a small flashlight. Derrick had gotten him a really cool plastic camera. It took tiny pictures that developed themselves. But the best present had come from his father. It was a set of books about pirates. The books were thick, with leather bindings, and full of illustrations.

"George?" came a voice from inside.

"Yeah, Dad?"

Peter van Gelder stepped outside. He was wearing the world's stupidest pirate costume: a black-and-white-striped shirt, a huge three-cornered hat, an eye patch, and a plastic sword hanging from his belt. His costume had been the only embarrassing thing about the party. True, George had been obsessed with pirates since he was a little kid. But he was eleven years old now. Somehow, Dad had never gotten the message that George was too old for costume birthday parties.

"I've got to go return this costume," his father said. "Will you kids be all right?"

"Yeah, sure."

"Okay," Peter van Gelder said. "See you in thirty-five minutes." He closed the door.

"Your dad's pretty cool, George," Shannon said when his footsteps had faded.

"Very funny," George answered.

"No, I mean it," she insisted. "He wore a better costume than Derrick or I did."

"I don't know about that," Derrick said, laughing. The orange streaks in Shannon's dark hair were Day-Glo. She went for a refined punk look in faded jeans and a bright red jacket, her guitar case by her side.

"Yeah, that's funny, Derrick," she said. "I'm serious, George. You said that your dad is boring, always reading musty old books. But he was so cool to throw this party—and he even dressed up as a pirate. You've got a thing about pirates, right?"

"I was really into them when I was little," he admitted reluctantly.

George took a deep breath. Shannon Starling

was one of the coolest kids in school. He had only
gotten to know her this year, and he felt a little
weird talking about his pirate obsession with her.
"Um, I still read about them sometimes."

"It's kind of sweet that he did the pirate thing,
then," Shannon went on. "Is it true that this used
to be a pirate's house?"

George glared at Derrick. Derrick must have
spilled the beans. It had been a long time since
he'd told anyone who had owned his house three
hundred years ago. George had learned as a little
kid that no one ever had believed him. They just
thought his pirate obsession was warping his
brain. "Thanks a lot, Derrick. Do you want me to
tell Shannon about your collection of—"

"Be quiet," Derrick interrupted, alarm in his
dark eyes. "Come on, George. It's no big deal.
You're always talking to me about it."

"About what?" Shannon asked.

She sounded like she really wanted to know.
George looked over his shoulder. His father was
long gone. But George wasn't sure who he was
really checking for. Sometimes he felt another presence in the house. Some nights it felt like the first
owner was still here, watching over his old home.

"Well, you know my house is really old," he
said, lowering his voice.

"Like, how old?" Shannon asked.

"Older than the United States."

Derrick snorted. "It's *in* the United States, George. How could it be older?"

"It was built more than three hundred years ago, back when New York was a British colony. You know, before the revolution."

"Tell her who built it," Derrick said.

"A famous pirate?" she asked.

"Well," George said. "Actually, he wasn't a pirate. He was a privateer. Which is like a pirate with a license."

"A pirate's license?" Derrick said. "What, did he have to take a test when he turned sixteen?"

"You guys are *so* making this up," Shannon said.

"Pirate, privateer, whatever," Derrick said. "Tell her *who*."

George looked over his shoulder again, feeling a familiar chill crawl up his spine. He lowered his voice even more, not wanting to say the name too loudly.

"Well, the name of the first owner of this house was . . . William Kidd . . . Captain Kidd."

"Whoa. *The* Captain Kidd?" Shannon whistled. "I've heard of him. Are you sure?"

"Yeah, I'm sure."

"How do you know?" Shannon asked.

"Because my mother was his wife's great-great-great-great-great-great-great-granddaughter." George counted them on his fingers.

"How many *greats* was that?" Derrick asked.

"Seven. She was my great-times-eight grand-mother."

"Wow. So you're practically a pirate yourself," Shannon said with a smirk.

"Not really," George explained. "We're only related by marriage. He married my many-times grandma, but he's not my ancestor by blood."

"Okay. That's enough of the family tree," Derrick said with a laugh.

But Shannon looked serious. "And the house has been in your family that long?" she asked. "There must be all kinds of cool old stuff here."

"Well, maybe in the attic. But I don't really go up there."

"What, are you kidding?" she asked. "You mean you've never been up there?"

George felt his cheeks turning red. "Well, of course I've been up there. Just . . . not very often."

He had been up there only once, actually, when he was five. It was just a few weeks after his mother had died. He'd followed his father up the stairs and knocked over a little pottery vase that his mother had given his father as a gift. The vase had shattered. That was when his dad had told him he wasn't allowed up there anymore. George had never talked to his dad about the attic since.

Shannon frowned. "I bet tons of pirate artifacts are up there."

"I doubt it. Just old papers and stuff."

"Like treasure maps?" Derrick asked.

"No, *boring* old papers. My dad's a history professor, not a treasure hunter. He's always talking about eastern European political conflicts—like when there were czars and disputes between noble families. Pretty boring stuff, if you ask me."

"I still don't get why you don't go up there," Shannon said.

George felt the color burn in his cheeks. "Well, I'm not supposed to. Some of the stuff is old, and some of it was my mom's."

"I think we should go check it out," Shannon insisted.

George bit his lip. It wasn't so much that he was scared of getting in trouble. It was something else that made him nervous to go in the attic.

"I don't know," he said.

"Come on," Shannon urged. "We'll be careful. Don't you want to see what's up there? You're in, right, Derrick?"

"Sure, why not?" Derrick responded.

"Okay, George. It's two against one," Shannon said. "Do we have to dare you?"

So that was it. Betrayed by his best friend, George had no choice. "Well . . . okay. We have to hurry, though," he said. "My dad's coming back in half an hour. And he's never late."

Shannon sprang to her feet. Derrick followed a little more slowly, having noticed George's apprehensive expression. The three of them went inside and to the stairs.

The moment George put his foot on the first step, the doorbell rang.

George jumped, instantly thinking his father had found him out—but his father wouldn't be ringing the bell to his own house. George crossed to the door and stood on tiptoe to look through the peephole.

"Happy birthday, George!"

George opened the door. It was Mr. Roulain, who lived in a big loft a few doors down. Mr. Roulain was one of the few adults George called a friend. He was the sort of guy who could talk to anyone. He and George's father had been friends for years. He always sounded sleepy, as if he had stayed up all night.

"I'm sorry I couldn't come to your party," Mr. Roulain said. "But I brought you a present."

"Oh, thanks," George said. He took the little package and opened it. "Wow!"

It was a watch. It glowed bright blue when George pressed a button on the side. It looked like the kind you could wear when diving to the bottom of the ocean. It had a stopwatch, an alarm, and best of all, a built-in compass.

"Now you'll never get lost, huh, George?"

"Thanks, Mr. Roulain. You're the best," George said. He strapped on the watch. It was one of the coolest presents he had gotten.

"Well, I have to go. I've got ice-hockey tickets, but happy birthday again. Tell your father I said hi."

The moment George closed the door, Shannon bounded up the stairs. "Come on," she said impatiently. George sighed and followed.

They reached the second floor, where George's room was. Only his father's room and the attic were above. Once they were past this point, they wouldn't have an excuse for being up here. And if his father came back while they were in the attic, there would be no way to sneak down.

George's house wasn't made for sneaking. The wooden floors all had creaky spots. The old windows moaned when it was windy. The whole house rattled as subway trains passed underneath. When George was little, he had believed that monsters lived in the basement, which was always damp and cold. The rumble of the subway trains and the hiss of steam pipes had turned into dragons and snakes in his dreams. But that was a long time ago.

George started up the narrow stairs to the third floor.

The faded wallpaper here was marked with a few bright rectangles outlining where pictures had once hung. After his wife died, Peter van Gelder had taken down all the pictures of her and the ones of them as a family. The rest of the house hadn't changed much in the last six years; but up here near his father's bedroom, it had become bare and lifeless—except for the ever-growing stacks of books.

Once they reached the top, George pointed silently at the ceiling where the door to the attic was visible. It was a trapdoor, which swung down with hinges from the ceiling.

"Move over," Shannon said. She jumped up and grabbed the cord that dangled from the door. The door folded down with the low creak of springs, the stairs dropping to the floor as if from the underside of a flying saucer.

"Cool," she said, grinning. She climbed the stairs and pushed open the door.

Derrick and George looked at each other.

Derrick's expression said it all. He didn't like getting in trouble, even with someone else's dad. George should have known Derrick would wimp out. He always did at the last minute. Oddly enough, now that George was this close, his nerves seemed to subside. He was even in the mood for a practical joke.

"Where do you think you're going?" George said, imitating his dad's authoritative voice.

"Don't do that," Shannon snapped, after she realized it had been George. "It gives me the creeps."

"She's right, George," Derrick said. "It isn't normal."

"It isn't normal." George mimicked Derrick perfectly. Imitating other voices was one of his special talents. His only special talent, really.

"That's a really bad habit," Derrick said.

"That's a really bad—"

"Shhh!" whispered Shannon as she disappeared into the attic.

George swallowed a laugh and looked up the stairs. His anticipation was growing. What if there really was some big secret up here? What if his father had discovered Captain Kidd's old papers? Maybe they'd been in the family for centuries. After all, it would be logical for Kidd to hide that stuff here. He'd lived in this house until he was sent to England and hanged. Maybe his father was hiding something, and that was why George wasn't allowed in the attic.

Come on. *His* father? Who was he kidding? George took a deep breath, climbed the stairs almost to the top, and looked around.

Shafts of sunlight streamed through a dirty skylight. The dark cherry-colored wood of the floor reflected the sun, making the whole room glow with red light. Pushed against the walls were old pieces of furniture—desks, a couple of heavy chests. George recognized a bedspread, a stack of sweaters, and an embroidered pillow. All of these things brought images of his mom flashing through his mind.

George stepped from the stairs, and Derrick scrambled up behind him.

"Should I fold up the stairs behind us?" Derrick asked.

Both Shannon and Derrick were looking at George like he was in charge now. As if this had been *his* idea. "No, keep the trapdoor open. I want to hear when my dad comes back."

"Wow. This furniture looks old. It must be the original stuff," Shannon said.

"Might be." George reached out his hand to touch the desk in front of him. If Shannon was right, it was more than three hundred years old. He put his palm against the sun-warmed wood. Somehow the desk felt right, like it really belonged here in the house. Like it had always been here.

Lying on it was a map. Not a treasure map, but an ordinary one with countries. George recognized that it was of the countries in eastern Europe—the nations his dad wrote all those papers about. But a shiver ran up George's spine when his fingers touched the date on the map—1697. That was weird. The map was from almost the same year as when the house had been built. So much had changed since then.

"Don't leave fingerprints!" whispered Derrick.

"What are you talking about? My dad's a history professor, not a detective."

"Still. We should be careful."

"You watch too many cop shows," Shannon said.

On the back of the desk was a rack of small square holes. Pigeonholes, George remembered they were called. Each one had a scroll of paper resting in it.

"Nice," Derrick said. "Maybe they're treasure maps!"

George pulled a scroll out carefully. He unrolled it, flinching when a tiny piece of paper crumbled from one corner. This stuff really was fragile. Maybe his dad was right, and he shouldn't be up here.

But he kept unrolling the paper.

It was written in fancy cursive, the ink blotchy and faded. He struggled to make out the words in the unfamiliar script.

Two boares, one hogshead of wheat, two flagons of ale . . .

"It sure is hard to read," Derrick grumbled.

"Let's see," George went on. "'Two boares . . . wheat . . . ale . . . ,' it sounds like a . . ." George couldn't bring himself to finish.

"Nice work, Sherlock!" Derrick said. "I believe you've discovered a shopping list." He put his hands over his mouth and snickered.

"A shopping list?" Shannon asked.

George dropped the document onto the desk. He had known what was probably up here. Boring stuff. Dad stuff. But it was a letdown to find out it was true.

"Look at this," Shannon said.

She was pointing at a painting high on the wall, a dark, somber portrait of a woman. She looked about thirty years old. George's jaw dropped.

"That's my mother," he said, astonished.

"George," Shannon said, "that painting's way too old to be of your mom."

"But it looks so much like her." George's hand

immediately reached for his pocket. Before she died, his mother had given him a locket. It was kind of a girlie thing—heart-shaped—so he kept it in his pocket instead of wearing it. He'd never even shown it to Derrick. But he always wanted it with him because it had her picture cut into ivory inside.

At least, he'd always *thought* it was his mother's picture.

He pulled the locket out and opened it. The face, the hair, the pose were all the same as the woman in the painting. The locket must be a lot older than he'd thought.

"Of course," George said as it hit him. "It's Sarah Oort."

Derrick looked over his shoulder at the locket. George tucked it back into his pocket hurriedly.

"Your great-great-great—?"

"Yes," George said. "My great-times-eight grandmother. The wife of Captain Kidd." The resemblance was so strong. The picture could easily have been his mother, only with slightly darker hair. His father never wanted pictures of his wife around, but this portrait looked so much like her. George wondered why his dad hadn't taken this one down.

"Look at the size of that diamond in her necklace!" Shannon said, whistling. Resting on the throat of the woman in the painting was a huge diamond.

"Whoa," George whispered, taking a step back.

"George!" Derrick said. "Watch out, you're—"

George felt himself bump into the desk behind him. He saw the eyes of the other two widen as he tried to brace himself. The shelf of pigeonholes toppled forward and crashed into him from behind, knocking him to the floor.

He was dazed for a second, staring at the ground. The weight of the rack was cutting into his shoulder.

"George, are you okay?" Shannon asked, sounding worried.

"Yeah, I think so." His shoulder hurt, but that was it. "Get this thing off me."

Shannon and Derrick lifted the grid from him. George stood shakily. He didn't feel like anything was broken, but he'd be sore tomorrow.

Then he saw the paper on the floor. It looked like a handful of dusty confetti.

"Uh-oh."

Little pieces had crumbled from the ancient documents when the shelf fell. Ancient bits covered the floor with paper snow. George looked at the desk. The scrolls were still there nestled in the pigeonholes. They hadn't completely disintegrated, but about a million little bits had fallen from them.

"We've got to get this cleaned up," Derrick hissed, kneeling down to scoop up the confetti. "Your dad's going to kill us!"

George knelt beside him and brushed the bits of paper into a pile. "Give us a hand, Shannon!"

"Shannon?" Derrick asked. "What's wrong?"

She was staring at the desk. A piece of wood had broken off the top.

"Great. How did I break that?" George said. He felt sick. This was major trouble.

"You didn't break it," Shannon answered. She turned to George. Her eyes were round with amazement. "But I think you found a treasure map."

Three

THE MAP TO FORTUNE

George and Derrick stood up, looking where Shannon pointed.

The desk wasn't broken after all, George saw with a surge of relief. A square wood panel—a secret panel—had popped up from its surface. The displacement of the panel had revealed a shallow cranny—a cranny that held a yellowed piece of paper. The paper lay flat, faceup. George looked at the strange marks on the page. Was it really a map? Or maybe some kind of diagram?

One thing was for certain—it wasn't a shopping list.

"What is it?" Derrick asked.

"I told you, it's a treasure map," Shannon insisted.

They both looked at George like he was some kind of expert.

"Well, it's obviously something important," he admitted. "I mean, it was hidden under this secret panel in the desk. But I don't know if it's a treasure map."

"It's a *secret* map, George," Shannon said. "In a house that was owned by a pirate. Do I really have to explain this to you guys?"

Derrick was staring at the map hard, looking at every notation from corner to corner. "It's not like any map I've ever seen. I mean, there aren't any coastlines or mountains or landmarks of any kind, just a bunch of lines and symbols."

"And you're some kind of expert?" Shannon scoffed. "I wonder if your dad knows how to read it, George."

"I wonder if he even knows it's *here*," George said. The panel had been invisible before the letter rack had crashed into the desk. The map, or whatever it was, could have been hidden for the last three hundred years.

He bent closer, studying the tattered paper. His heartbeat quickened as he saw some letters in the upper-right corner. "Whoa. Look!" he said. " 'W. K.'!"

"Is that some kind of abbreviation?" Derrick asked. "For *week*? Or *Western* something?"

"Try William Kidd," George said. His voice shook. "As in *Captain* Kidd."

"See? See?" Shannon's voice rose with excitement. "I told you!"

"Uh, guys, do you hear that?" Derrick asked.

George froze—and heard the door downstairs opening.

He looked at his new watch. Seven o'clock exactly. He felt sweat breaking out all over him.

Derrick pointed down at the scattered bits of paper on the floor. He and Shannon knelt down to scoop it hurriedly into their hands.

"Where?" Derrick whispered.

Shannon stuck the paper into her jacket pockets, and Derrick silently did the same.

"Get the map!" Shannon said in a fierce whisper.

George went to grab the map from its nook inside the desk. But as his fingers poked into the compartment, something terrible happened.

As he fumbled for the map, George's finger knocked into the wooden lid to the compartment, and suddenly George heard a *click*. When he looked over, he saw that the lid had reattached to the compartment—it was closed again, with the map inside!

"Uh-oh," George muttered.

"George, I'm home!" Peter van Gelder's voice echoed from downstairs.

"Come on, George!" Shannon whispered. "Get the map—we have to go!"

George reached for the lid and pulled, but it wouldn't budge. The compartment was locked tight!

"I think I locked it again!" George whispered. He kept pulling at the wooden lid, straining to hear his dad moving around downstairs. What if he was climbing the steps already? What if he was right outside the attic door . . . ?

"Can you open it?" Derrick whispered.

George pulled and pulled, trying to pry the lid loose with his fingernails, but he wasn't making any progress. "It won't open," he whispered through clenched teeth.

"George?"

George moaned. His dad's voice was definitely getting closer.

"We don't have time," Shannon said. She scooped the rest of the confetti into her pockets.

George's eyes frantically swept the attic. The paper scrolls in their pigeonholes didn't look too much the worse for wear. "The attic looks okay," he said. "We have to go. Maybe we can come back for the map another time."

"Don't worry," Derrick whispered. "I memorized it."

"You what?"

"I memorized the map."

George rolled his eyes. Derrick was always going on about his photographic memory. George doubted there was any such thing, but for now, they just had to get moving. His dad was on his way upstairs.

They headed for the attic steps. Derrick peeked down, then descended. The stairs creaked as George went down. Shannon stepped off the last slat and lifted the lower tier of the staircase from the ground in one smooth motion. Springs and gears ground noisily as she folded the stairs back up into the ceiling.

"George?"

It was his father's voice again. He was definitely on the second floor. They were trapped up here.

George and Derrick looked at each other helplessly. George never came up to the third floor. All that was up here was his father's room and a bathroom.

"Up here, Mr. van Gelder," Shannon yelled.

What was she thinking? George opened his mouth to protest, but it was too late.

As Peter van Gelder climbed toward them, George saw something moving out of the corner of his eye. It was the cord that pulled down the attic stairs. It was swinging wildly. There was no way his dad could miss it. Shannon reached up to the cord and brought it to a stop with two fingers, then dropped her hand to her side.

George's dad came into view, his eyes narrowed with curiosity.

"You have a really nice house, Mr. van Gelder," Shannon said quickly.

"Uh, thank you, Shannon."

"George was just showing me the whole thing," she continued cheerily. "I hope you don't mind. I never met anyone in New York City who owned a whole house before."

"Well, it's been in my wife's family a long—"

"All of my friends live in apartments. Except my friend Josephine, whose parents have a brown-stone. But that's way out in Brooklyn."

Peter van Gelder opened his mouth, then closed it again. He looked a bit overwhelmed by Shannon's rapid-fire talk. She brushed past him, and Derrick and George followed. They had made it. They hadn't been caught.

But George hardly even cared. All he could think about was the paper in the secret compartment. The paper with Captain Kidd's initials on it.

After Shannon left, George and Derrick helped clean up the mess from the party. It wasn't until George had come back from taking out the last load of trash with his dad that he realized Derrick had disappeared. George walked around the first floor, then headed for his room. There he found Derrick sitting on his bed, drawing something on the back of a piece of wrapping paper.

"What are you doing?" George asked.

Derrick turned the paper around to show George.

George's eyes widened. "Whoa!"

On the paper was a copy of the map they'd seen up in the attic. As far as George could tell, all the odd intersecting lines were there. And the words. It looked exactly the same.

"How did you do that?"

"I told you, I have a photographic memory—or something close to it. If I really look at something, I can remember it."

"I thought you were just making that up," George confessed.

Derrick raised one eyebrow as he handed George the map. "Happy birthday."

Four

PHOTOGRAPHIC PROOF

On Monday, George couldn't pay attention in school. He had hardly slept the night before. Questions had raced through his mind as he lay staring at the ceiling. He could still see the attic, the picture of his distant ancestor, and the hidden map. He wondered how close Derrick's copy of the map was to the original.

All morning, he stared out of the classroom window and thought about the things he had noticed on Derrick's map. He could hardly wait to decipher more, to find out how close they were to the buried treasure.

When the lunch bell finally rang, he met Shannon and Derrick at their usual table.

Shannon looked exhausted. "Okay," she said as she sat down, "I tried to put the bits of paper back together all night. No way. They just turned into dust. I couldn't tell which pieces were the shopping list."

"It's okay, Shannon," Derrick said. "We've got

what counts." He glanced at George. "Show her."

George took the map from his pocket and placed it on the table before Shannon.

She frowned at it, then turned it over. The paper Derrick had used had been the wrapping for Mr. Roulain's gift. It was a circus clown pattern. They were riding unicycles and carrying birthday cakes.

"You guys are kidding, right?" she said. "This is supposed to be a copy?"

George could tell Derrick was about to get defensive. "Derrick has a photographic memory— at least close to it," he explained.

"The copy is perfect," Derrick said. "A genuine replica. I guarantee it's exactly the same as the original."

"Besides, it's all we've got," George added. "I don't know if I'll ever be able to get that desk open again. And I'd have to wait until my dad's not around to even try."

"But how can we be sure this map is the same as the original? What if it's only, you know, *almost* right?" Shannon asked. "We could be standing ten feet from the treasure and miss it completely!"

"The copy is perfect!" Derrick repeated, louder this time.

Derrick and Shannon glared at each other. George realized he had to calm things down. If

Derrick's copy was as good as he claimed, they might be able to find a real treasure. But Shannon was also right. It would be crazy to follow a map if they weren't positive it was right.

"Okay, both of you chill out," he said. "Let's do a test."

"What kind of test?"

"A test of Derrick's memory."

Derrick stared at him through skeptical eyes for a moment, then nodded.

"Okay, I'm game."

George pointed to one of Shannon's textbooks. Sixth-grade science. "Can I borrow that?"

Shannon's eyes lit up. "Good idea," she said. "But I get to pick the page."

George swallowed. He hoped she didn't pick a page that was too complicated.

"Whatever," Derrick said. "But find a diagram. Not just a bunch of words."

"No problem." Shannon leafed through the book. She was looking at the very end of the text, the chapters they hadn't gotten to yet. Derrick sat back with his hands clasped behind his head, a relaxed smile on his face. Finally, Shannon laid the book flat on the table, turned it to face the two boys, and slid it across.

"Thirty seconds," she said.

"Twenty," Derrick answered. He stared at the book with furious concentration.

George looked at the diagram. It was labeled THE WATER CYCLE. It showed water moving around in a big circle. The water evaporated from the ocean, went up into the clouds, then rained onto the land. It tumbled down mountains and into rivers and wound up flowing back into the ocean. It seemed pretty straightforward, but there were a lot of little details and a lot of big words. A lot of things that Derrick could get wrong. George hoped that this test wouldn't just start another argument.

George had hardly had any time to think these thoughts when Shannon looked up from her watch. She reached across and shut the book with a snap.

Derrick smiled up at her and opened his notebook. He began to draw.

George and Shannon ate their lunches in silence. It was Shannon's turn to look relaxed now, smiling as if she were about to win a bet. Derrick bent over his notebook, the expression of concentration still on his face. George chewed his sandwich nervously.

After five minutes, Derrick looked up from his work. He shook a cramp from his hand, then turned the notebook around to Shannon.

"Read it and weep."

Her eyes widened as she studied Derrick's drawing. She opened the textbook to compare.

George went around to Shannon's side of the table and looked over her shoulder.

"Whoa," he said, his eyes darting back and forth between the textbook and the notebook. "All right, Derrick!" The whole diagram was there—the wavy lines of water evaporating, the fluffy clouds and spiky mountains, even the six little trees beside one of the rivers, which were just there for decoration. The labels were all there, too, even the artist's name at the bottom of the drawing.

After a minute, Shannon shut the textbook.

"You spelled *erosion* wrong," she said

Derrick closed his eyes and tilted his head upward for a second. Then he shook his head. "No, I didn't."

"True," Shannon said softly. "Just testing. You spelled everything right."

George sat back down next to Derrick. He looked at his friend with a new respect. He knew that Derrick never had to study much for tests and always got good grades, but he hadn't realized the guy was a *freak*.

"Okay," Shannon admitted. "I guess we have a treasure map!"

They spent the rest of lunch studying the map and planning.

"Hey, look what it says here!" George said.

"'*Canis Marinus,*'" Shannon read out. "Huh. I'm not sure, but it sounds like Latin."

"Weird," Derrick said. "What do you think it means?"

"It means 'Sea Dog,'" George said proudly.

Shannon frowned at him. "Sea dog? How do you know that?"

"It's the name of our house," George explained. "Back in Captain Kidd's day, New York wasn't big enough to need numbers for every house. They used names instead. Captain Kidd named his house *Canis Marinus*, or Sea Dog. There's still a tile on our house's foundation with the name and a little picture of a ship."

"Cool," said Shannon.

George nodded. "Of course, now we have a number, too: one eighteen Windsor Lane."

Derrick pointed at the map. "Look what it says down here at the lower left: '*S.O.*'"

"What could that be?" Shannon asked.

George thought for a moment. "It's probably Sarah Oort, my ancestor. Captain Kidd's wife."

"Wait," Derrick said, scratching his head through his dark, curly hair. "If she's your great-something grandmother, isn't Kidd your great-something grandfather?"

"No, I'm not related to him at all," George said. "How come with your supermutant memory you keep forgetting this?"

Derrick sighed. "It's a *photographic* memory. Telling me stuff doesn't do much good. You've got to show me a picture."

"Whatever. Just listen," George explained. "William Kidd was Sarah Oort's third husband. They didn't have any children. But after William Kidd was hanged for piracy, Sarah Oort married another man, Ulysses Pyle. *He's* my great-times-eight grandfather."

"So what's the story? Why was Kidd hung if he had a pirate's license?" Derrick asked.

"It was called a charter. The king of England gave it to Kidd. It allowed him to attack ships from certain countries, like France, or other enemies of England. Then Kidd was supposed to split the bounty between himself, his investors, and the king. Kidd was hanged for breaking the charter."

"So he broke the rules?" Shannon said.

"That's what they claimed at his trial. He attacked a ship he wasn't supposed to. But it wasn't Kidd's fault—the other ship was flying a flag that made it look like it belonged to an enemy even though it didn't. It's really complicated. I think the people who invested in his ship just decided they wanted to keep his share of the treasure."

Derrick frowned. "So they hung—uh, *hanged* him to steal his share of the money?"

"Yeah. I read this book that explained how the whole trial was fixed," George explained. "They didn't let him say anything in his defense. He just had to sit there and listen."

"They could do that?" Shannon asked.

"They could do anything. A lot of important people were investors. People who could make their own rules."

"That's totally unfair," Derrick said indignantly.

"He must have had some really cool treasure," Shannon remarked.

"And the king wanted to get Kidd out of the way and keep the treasure for his royal self," Derrick said. "So Kidd got royally framed."

"Does anyone know what the treasure was?" Shannon asked.

George shook his head. "Not for sure. But there were lots of rumors that the ship Kidd captured on his last voyage was carrying something incredibly valuable—and that's why he was killed."

"Like chests full of gold coins," Derrick suggested.

"Or pieces of eight," Shannon said. "Or jewels!"

Visions of glittering mountains of gems danced in front of George's eyes. "It could be anything. No one ever found Kidd's last haul. Some people say there was nothing to find. But a lot of people think that there was—and that Kidd hid it before he was captured—maybe even somewhere in New York."

"And this map shows where!" Shannon said. Her eyes were shining. "What if we really find it? We'll be rich! Just think about it!"

"Yeah!" Derrick put his chin in his hands, a dreamy expression on his face. "Man, if I had a chest full of gold, I'd buy a giant flat-screen TV for every room in my family's apartment. Oh, and I'd buy us a bigger apartment so I wouldn't have to share a room with my little brother. Wait—why an apartment? Why not a whole house? And—"

"Wait, wait," George broke in. "Slow down. We haven't found the treasure yet, remember? We haven't even figured out how to read this map."

"Oh, yeah." Derrick blinked. "Right. Okay. So . . . what's this number here?" he asked, pointing at the map.

"'MDCXCIX'?" Shannon read out. "That's . . . uh . . . sixteen hundred ninety-nine."

"I think that's the year the map was drawn. Sixteen ninety-nine," George said. He'd thought about this last night. He looked at Shannon and Derrick. "It also was the year Kidd was sent to England for his trial."

Shannon wrinkled her forehead. "Is that important?"

"It could be," George said. Excitement bubbled up in him again. "What if Kidd hid the treasure right before his trial? Maybe he knew they were coming for him, and he buried it so his enemies wouldn't get it."

"Wow," Shannon whispered.

They all looked at the map with new excitement. It was still just a bunch of lines, squiggles, and mysterious symbols. But it might hold the clues to finding a secret treasure—a treasure worth dying for.

There was only one sentence on the map. "'The key to good fortune lies in the heart,'" George read.

"That's kind of sweet," Shannon said. "But what does it mean?"

"What does *any* of it mean?" Derrick said, frowning.

They both looked at George. He thought about admitting that he'd never actually seen a pirate's map before. The only map he had ever really studied was the New York subway map. But between the three of them he *was* the expert on pirates. He had to at least sound like he knew what he was saying.

He licked his lips. "Well," he said. "Here's an X."

"As in, 'X marks the spot,'" Shannon said. "Buried treasure."

"Okay," Derrick said. "I see the X on the map. But where is it in real life?"

George pointed at the map. "See this square here? It's right under *Canis Marinus*."

"The square is your house, right?" Shannon said.

"Probably."

Shannon frowned at the map. "There's a skull and crossbones inside. What do you think that means?"

George shrugged. "I dunno. It's kind of freaky. Maybe we'll figure it out when we start looking around. See this wavy line underneath? It leads away from my house. It goes to the right and kind of angles down."

Shannon shrugged. "Right probably means east and down is probably south, don't you think?"

"But south of your house is Wall Street. Huge skyscrapers. With really deep foundations," Derrick added with a shake of his head.

"Oh," Shannon said.

They all were silent for a moment. In the last three

hundred years, New York City had completely trans-
formed from a colonial town into a major metropolis.
Buildings that soared into the sky had been built,
torn down, rebuilt. Landfill had been added to make
solid ground where water had been in Kidd's day.
Chances are, any buried treasure had been dug up or
accidentally destroyed a long time ago.

"This doesn't look good," Shannon said. "I
mean, how much of downtown Manhattan is the
same as it was three centuries ago?"

"Pretty much only my street," George said. "All
the houses on Windsor Lane were protected as
historical landmarks. You can't even paint them
without permission."

"What if down doesn't mean south?" Derrick
said suddenly.

"What else would it mean?" Shannon asked.

"What if down means *down*? What if that's what
the wavy line means?"

George's eyebrows rose. He thought of the subways rumbling under his house, the hissing steam
pipes that descended deep into the ground.

"There are a lot of tunnels in Manhattan," he said.

"Yeah, but those weren't built way back then,
were they?" Shannon said. "I mean, pirates didn't
take the subway to work."

"But a lot of tunnels are made by old streams,"

Derrick said. "There's a fountain in the lobby of my building. The doorman says that it's fed by a stream that was there when the building was built. They paved over it, but the water cuts its own tunnel, no matter how much you try to stop it up." He glanced at Shannon. "It's called erosion. *E-r-o-s-i-o-n.*"

Shannon rolled her eyes. "Okay, okay."

"So maybe this wavy line is a tunnel?" George asked. "You know, my basement is always damp and smells moldy. Maybe it's from an underground stream."

"And maybe that created a tunnel, and Kidd knew about it," Shannon said.

George felt a flicker of doubt. "What are we supposed to do? Dig up my basement?"

"Wait. Look at this little symbol here," Derrick said.

At the bottom of the map, between the house and the wavy line, was an eight-sided shape.

"What's that, a stop sign?" Shannon asked.

George shook his head. "I don't think they had stop signs back then."

"Well, maybe it's a door," Shannon said.

"There's no door in my basement."

Shannon cracked her knuckles and leaned back. "Not that you *know* about."

Five

OPERATION: BRIDGE NIGHT

For once, George was glad his dad was predictable. That would make it easier to keep the plan a secret. Tuesday night was bridge night. Every week, George's dad played cards with the St. Johns, the British couple who lived next door. Since the game was only one house away, George had convinced his dad years ago that a baby-sitter was a waste of money.

At seven o'clock, the usual time, Peter van Gelder came to George's room to say good night.

"I'll see you tomorrow. Remember, lights out at ten. Call if you need anything."

"No problem, Dad." George smiled up from his math book, trying to look relaxed. It was hard—he'd been so keyed up about searching for Kidd's treasure that he'd barely slept or eaten since he'd found the map.

"Is your schoolwork going okay?"

"Yeah. Fine." George clasped his hands over the open book, waiting for his father to leave.

Peter van Gelder shifted his feet. George recognized the signs and bit back a groan. His father wanted to *talk*. Normally, George would have been happy—he loved the rare occasions when he and his dad actually had real conversations. Usually, Peter van Gelder seemed too hurried, too much in his own world to relax and just talk about *stuff*.

"Hey, did you get a chance yet to crack those books I gave you?" Peter van Gelder pointed at the leather-bound pirate books on George's desk.

"Oh, yeah. They're, uh, they're really great," George said. "Maybe I'll have more time to read them this weekend." George had already gone through the chapters on William Kidd—twice. He'd searched the index for anything about buried treasure, as well. George wanted to tell his dad more about how much he liked the books, but Shannon and Derrick would be at the door in fifteen minutes. Why did his dad want to talk at the most inconvenient times?

Peter van Gelder paused a moment, waiting for more, then sighed softly.

"Okay, lights out at ten."

"Got it."

His father went downstairs. A few minutes later, George heard the front door close. He slammed the math book shut and ran downstairs.

At seven-fifteen exactly, the doorbell rang. He was already waiting at the door.

"You brought your *guitar*?" he asked as Shannon and Derrick pushed in past him.

"Not exactly," Shannon answered. "This is just cover." She plopped the guitar case on the floor, grunting like it weighed a ton.

"Oh, man!" George said when she opened the case.

It was full of shovels, a hoe, and a pick that looked like it was for mountain climbing. When the last piece of equipment clunked onto the floor, Shannon said, "Let's go."

"Where did you get all that stuff?" George asked. "You don't have a garden."

"You know Renee, the Diversions' drummer? She and her parents are way into the outdoors. She let me borrow this."

"But we're not going to dig up my whole basement, are we? I think my dad might notice a gaping hole down there."

"Hmmm," she said, as if the idea had never occurred to her. George got the feeling that Shannon would be happy to tear down the whole house if she thought there was treasure to be found.

"Relax, George," Derrick said. "We won't dig until we're sure." He pulled a long device out of the guitar case. It had a disk on the end. It looked sort of like a vacuum cleaner.

"What on earth is that?" George asked.

Derrick flicked a switch on the device and shoved it toward George. He waved it up and down George's body. When it got to his waist, it beeped.

George jumped back.

"Are you wearing a belt with a big buckle?"

George pulled up his shirt, revealing his silver belt buckle. "Is that a metal detector?"

"Yep," Derrick said. "My granddad uses it to find change and stuff on the beach. I figured I could borrow it for some real treasure hunting."

"So we'll know exactly where to dig," Shannon said. "We'll hit the secret door on the first try. Metal stuff should be right behind it."

"Right," said George, feeling more and more nervous. "Or we'll hit a steam pipe or some electric cables . . ."

"Or bars of gold," Derrick said. "Let's go."

"Your basement *is* damp," Shannon said. "And creepy."

There was one bare bulb, and its light hardly stretched beyond the center of the room.

George shivered, crossing his arms over his chest. It was a warm night outside in New York.

The spring sunshine had baked the streets and buildings all day. But down here, the damp chill seemed to reach straight into his bones.

"Maybe that means there's an underground stream," Derrick said. He was sweeping the metal detector slowly over the concrete floor. So far, it had beeped for a quarter, an old key, and a couple pieces of wire. But not for any secret doors.

"Hey, what if it's a river? Can everyone swim?" George asked. He was trying to control a rising feeling of nervousness.

"Well, it wouldn't really be a river. Just a stream," Derrick said as he swiped the metal detector through a corner. "I asked my doorman. He says there are old springs everywhere in Manhattan. I guess there are underground streams everywhere, too."

He finished sweeping the metal detector over the last corner of the basement. "Huh. That's it, I guess. No door."

The three stood there in silence for a moment. The buzz of the tiny light in the ceiling was the only sound. The shapes of discarded boxes and old sports equipment made weird shadows on the walls. George had never liked the basement, but now he hated it. He felt ripped off—it was just a wet, smelly basement after all.

"Maybe you did it too fast," Shannon said. "You could have missed a spot."

A low rumbling filled the basement as a subway train approached. "Or maybe the door's under one of these piles of boxes," George said, suddenly unwilling to give in. Derrick had only covered the parts of the basement floor that were easy to get to. There was still a lot of floor that was covered by boxes, a table saw, a couple of rusted bicycles—stuff that had always been there, as far as George knew.

"Which means we have to do some real work." Shannon groaned and walked over to one of the piles of boxes. "Derrick, you go over the floor again in case you missed anything, and George and I will clear this stuff away."

George joined Shannon at the boxes and struggled to shift them to another corner. When they were halfway done, they took a break.

"Man, these are heavy," he gasped.

"No kidding. What's in them, bricks?"

George opened one of the boxes. Under the flaps was a clear plastic sheet. He poked around until he found an opening in the plastic and reached in.

"Books," he said.

"I think bricks would be lighter," Shannon said, grunting as she slid another box across the concrete.

George pulled one of the books from the box. It was heavy and leather-bound, without any words on its black cover. It smelled like an old library, musty and ancient. He opened the book to its title page.

"*'A History of the New York Waterfront,'*" he read out loud.

"Hey, History Boy, we've gotta keep moving," Shannon said.

George ignored her and pulled out another thick book. It was called *New York Underground*.

"These must be my mom's old books," he said. "They're all histories of New York City. These could come in handy."

George's mother had also been a history professor. She'd studied New York colonial history, when the city had been a Dutch and then a British outpost. George wondered what she'd been doing with these books about modern developments like the subway system.

"I'm sure they're enlightening," Shannon said. "But we have to find that secret door first."

"Okay, okay." George knew she was right. They only had so much time. He put the two books back under the plastic and looked at all the boxes. *There must be* hundreds *of books down here,* he thought. *Anything you wanted to know about*

New York could probably be found in this basement.

George closed the flaps and carried the box over to Shannon. She was making a new pile in one of the corners Derrick had already checked with his metal detector. As they moved boxes, the basement was filled with the shuffle of feet and the swish of cardboard sliding on concrete.

Finally, only one huge box remained to be moved. It was enormous.

Shannon and George looked at each other.

"You get that side," she commanded. "One, two, three . . ."

They lifted the box a few inches above the ground, groaning as they shuffled a few feet.

"I think I'm going to—" George cried, feeling the box slip under his fingers.

"Me too!"

The box dropped to the floor with a *thunk*. George rubbed his back and moaned. He'd never lifted anything so heavy. Suddenly, the basement didn't seem so cold, but it was still wet. Sweat dripped into his eyes and down his neck.

"Maybe you guys should just slide it," Derrick suggested.

Shannon didn't say anything. She was kneeling beside the box, bent close to where the wall and floor met.

"You okay, Shannon?" George asked.

Without answering, she suddenly turned toward the box and pushed wildly. Her feet scrabbled on the concrete. The box didn't budge. "Help me move this!" she ordered frantically.

George quickly knelt beside her and braced his feet against the wall. He put his hands on the box and shoved it as hard as he could.

The box finally moved, and Shannon kept it going across the floor. When it reached the middle of the basement, she turned around, gasping.

"Congratulations," Derrick said. "I think you just invented a new Olympic sport."

"Oh, yeah?" Shannon said, standing up. She fumbled in her pocket and pulled out a small flashlight. She shone it on the wall next to where George still knelt. "So do I get a gold medal for *this*?"

George and Derrick looked at the circle of light on the wall. The flashlight's beam disappeared into a ragged hole about a foot and a half across.

"Wow!" George said. He'd lived in this house all his life, and he'd never seen the hole. The stack of boxes had always covered it. His muscles still ached from the lifting, but he rushed forward with renewed excitement.

"I guess I'd give that a ten," Derrick said.

George looked into the hole. It appeared to go

on forever. The darkness seemed to swallow the little beam of Shannon's flashlight. He reached one hand inside cautiously. It was even colder inside the gap, the air damp and still. He placed his hand flat on the floor. It was smooth and grainy.

"Wow, the floor's just dirt in there!" he said. "The concrete stops at the edge of the wall."

"Can you see anything?"

He shook his head. "No."

Shannon scuttled over next to him and poked the flashlight into the hole. George struggled to peer past her. He could see another wall only a few feet away. The wall was made of old irregular stones held together by mortar.

George tried to hide his disappointment. For a moment he'd thought the hole would lead to another world, not just a small compartment. "I guess that's the original wall of the house," he said.

Shannon dropped to the floor and shimmied through the hole. The flashlight swung wildly inside the gap. George blinked as her feet disappeared.

"Shannon?"

"Cool! I can stand up in here."

George knelt at the hole again. He could see only her feet and ankles.

"How big is it?"

"Like a closet. Three feet deep. Maybe four feet wide. It seems to go pretty high, though."

George thought about the shape of his house. Why would there be a little room that jutted out like this? He looked at the watch Mr. Roulain had given him, checking the compass. The hole was on the north side of the house. George peered up, trying to picture what was above his and Shannon's heads. They were standing under the back of the house, right under . . .

"The chimney!" he said.

"What?" Shannon's voice was muffled.

"You're right under the fireplace in the living room."

"That would explain the smell."

"Why do you have a fireplace in the basement?" Derrick asked.

"Maybe this wasn't the basement back then," George said. "Maybe the street level used to be lower."

"Well," Shannon's voice came from inside the chimney, "whatever it is, there's a dirt floor. Let's dig."

"Wait. Let's try this first," Derrick said. He shoved the head of the metal detector into the gap. It disappeared into the hole.

A shrill beep rang out with an almost constant pitch. They looked at one another, their mouths open.

Shannon's face appeared. Her cheeks were smudged with dirt, but she was grinning broadly. "Give me a shovel!"

The dirt floor of the chimney was packed down hard. George wondered how long it had been since anyone had been there. It didn't seem like it could have been three hundred years. The dirt broke freely when Shannon pounded it with the edge of the shovel. *Someone* had dug here before.

After a while, Shannon got tired and crawled out. She looked like she'd spent a week in the woods without a tent or even a sleeping bag. Her clothes were covered with dirt, her face streaked with sooty sweat.

"Someone else's turn," she said tiredly.

"Let me," George said. He'd dreamed his whole life of discovering something of Captain Kidd's in this house. A little bit of dirt wasn't going to stop him. The treasure could be just a few feet away.

George got down on the floor. Shannon handed him the flashlight, and he clutched it in one fist. He crawled slowly into the hole.

It was dark and cool. The ground, broken up by Shannon's work, was no longer smooth. The pieces were sharp, like shards of stone. He drew in his feet and stood up.

Shining the flashlight around, he could see that all four walls were made of stone. For a moment, George just stood and breathed in the air. As he had grown up in the house, he'd often wondered if he was standing in a spot where Captain Kidd had been three hundred years before. Now he felt strangely certain that he was standing in Kidd's footprints.

George rested the flashlight in one corner, pointed at the center of the floor. He lifted the shovel and thrust it down as hard as he could. A few pieces of the hard-packed dirt broke away. He kicked them over into the pile of dirt in another corner, then banged the shovel down again. Only a single chunk of dirt broke loose.

Again and again, he thrust the shovel into the dirt. The pile in the corner grew—but slowly, slowly.

George was inside the chimney for what seemed like an hour. Big blisters burned on both his palms. He could barely see in the flashlight's weak glow. Occasionally, a subway train would pass by, and the whole chimney would tremble as if the house above were about to collapse. The air would shake. Then it was calm, the weight of centuries-old stone upon him. The sounds of his breathing and the *clank* of the shovel filled the chimney space.

When the shovel finally struck something hard, it took him a moment to remember where he really was.

He tested the spot again. A hollow boom sounded. His heart skipped a beat. He picked up the flashlight and pointed it down at the spot, scooping away dirt with his other hand.

"I hit something," he said, trying to sound calm.

"What? What?" Shannon and Derrick both yelped.

"It looks like a piece of wood."

Shannon and Derrick's faces crowded into the hole. They stared at the place where the flashlight pointed. George brushed away more dirt.

"Wow, you found it!" Shannon cried.

"Here." Derrick handed a smaller shovel through.

George forgot about his blisters as he went back to work, attacking the packed dirt. In less than five minutes, he had cleared the entire door.

It was only about two and a half feet square. The planks of wood were blackened with age. In its center, a doorknob stuck up.

"Look at the knob," Shannon gasped, her head shoved into the chimney shaft. "It has eight sides."

George nodded. It was shaped just like the symbol at the bottom of the map. This door had to lead to the treasure!

"Open it!" Derrick cried.

George took a deep breath and grasped the

knob with both hands. He planted his feet at both sides of the door and pulled.

The door didn't budge.

George could see dirt packed into the seams around the frame of the door. It obviously hadn't been opened for a long time. He shifted his feet and grasped the knob again. He pulled harder this time, rocking back and forth. The wooden planks began to creak. He felt the door start to loosen.

Then, with a *crack,* it swung up at him.

George flailed. His arms swung back as he bumped his head against the wall of the chimney space. One foot slipped into the blackness that had suddenly opened under him. Dirt skittered down through the door.

"Whoa!" he shouted. He heard an echo of his own voice from the open doorway.

He slid backward and pulled his foot onto solid ground. Derrick slithered halfway into the chimney shaft, the flashlight in his hand. "You okay?"

"I'm fine," George said breathlessly. He'd almost plunged down into total darkness—but that wasn't why his heart was banging against his ribs.

It was because he'd actually opened Captain Kidd's secret trapdoor.

They were one step closer to finding the treasure!

Six

On the Edge

"I wonder how deep this hole is." Derrick put his head over the edge and pointed the flashlight downward.

George looked past his friend's head, his eyes following the ray of light. "Jeez," he whispered. He couldn't see the bottom.

Shannon pushed her way in, and the three of them peered into the hole.

"George, do you realize you almost *fell* down there?" Derrick asked.

"Yeah, I kind of noticed that." George still had the almost-falling feeling in his gut. His hands would still be shaking if he weren't clutching the edge of the hole so tightly.

"Wow," Shannon said. Her voice echoed back from the bottom of the hole. "You'd be so dead."

George gave a shaky laugh. "Thanks, Shannon."

"I thought there would be stairs or something," Derrick said.

"Come on, it's a door that leads to pirate treasure,"

George said. "The point of burying it is to make it hard to get."

George didn't mention all the other ways pirates protected their treasure. Booby traps. False maps. Corpses buried along with the treasure so that the ghosts of the dead men would guard it.

Captain Kidd probably never did any of *those* things, though. He had been a privateer, not a pirate. Most of the history books agreed on that. *Most* of them.

"This hole looks deep," Shannon said. "How did they build something like this way back then?"

"They probably didn't," George said. "The hole was probably made by natural forces. The house was just built on top of it."

"How deep do you think it is?" Derrick asked.

George dug a nickel from his pocket and dropped it. He counted, "One, two, three . . ." and then heard a wet plonk from below.

"That was a splash!" Shannon said.

George nodded. Derrick must have been right about old rivers carving out tunnels in New York. George pointed the flashlight down again. This time, his eyes caught the glimmer of water below.

"Well, it's not *that* deep," he said. "Not like a mile or anything."

"So, we just need to get some rope," Shannon said. "Do you have any?"

Derrick and George looked at her. All three of them were covered with dirt and exhausted from digging and moving boxes around the basement.

"As in *right now*?" Derrick said. He looked at his watch. "It's after nine. My mom will be here to pick me up in a half hour."

"Are you kidding?" Shannon cried. "We're right here. We could be looking at the treasure five minutes from now! How can you think of leaving?"

"I have a soccer game tomorrow. I can't play if I break my leg falling into some pit."

George swallowed. It was hard not to agree with Shannon, but . . . "Derrick's right. You guys have to go soon, and we need to be more prepared. We need more than rope. We've got to get other climbing stuff to make it safe. Who knows what's down there?"

"We need a bigger flashlight," Derrick said. "*Three* bigger flashlights."

"All right, all right." Shannon groaned. "But when are we going down?"

George thought about it. "My dad's going to be out Saturday afternoon."

"*Saturday?*"

"That's only four days away, Shannon," Derrick said. "This hole's been here for three hundred years. It's not going anywhere."

"Okay," she said at last. "But you guys have to promise not to go down there without me."

George shook his head. The thought of going down into the hole alone gave him the creeps. He'd never liked dark, enclosed spaces. But more than that, it would just be wrong to go ahead without both Shannon and Derrick. In the pirate stories he'd read, whenever someone double-crossed a member of his crew, bad things happened.

"Don't worry," he said. "There's no way we're going anywhere without you. In fact, I think we should all take an oath to do this together."

"Good idea," Shannon said. "Let's do it now!" She spat into her hand and held it out.

"Ewww!" said Derrick.

"Swear!"

It wasn't exactly what he'd had in mind. But George spat into his own hand.

"The treasure is for all of us. No one goes after it alone, no one gets it for him- or herself," Shannon said. "Come on, Derrick. Swear."

Derrick sighed, then spat into his palm. They all stuck out their hands.

"Okay, what are we supposed to do now?" Shannon asked George.

George thought fast, then put his hand out over the hole, palm up. "Derrick?"

Derrick put his hand on top of George's with a grimace. Then Shannon put her hand on top of Derrick's.

"Ewww. I'm in a spit sandwich!" Derrick said.

George bit his lip. "Okay, repeat after me. . . . Um . . . we all swear on this secret door."

"We all swear on this secret door," they repeated.

George thought of all the betrayals he had read about. Pirates fought over their treasure, mutinied, stranded one another on deserted islands. He tried to think of a pirate oath he'd read, but he couldn't, so he made one up. "We swear that none of us will go down through this door unless we all go through the door. And that we'll share everything we find down there equally."

As Derrick and Shannon repeated the words, George thought of one more sentence to add.

"And we will never leave anyone behind."

"Agreed," said Shannon. "Everyone comes up."

"No problem with that," said Derrick. "I swear."

The hinges creaked as they closed the secret door. Derrick and Shannon packed up the shovels, hoe, and pick, then stowed the guitar case inside the chimney base. Then they pushed the boxes of books back in front of the hole in the wall. George swept the dirt that was now all over the basement floor. By the time they were done, the basement looked the same as it always had, but cleaner. Now that the door was hidden again, it was hard for George to believe they'd found a three-hundred-year-old tunnel here, right under his own house.

"I'll borrow some climbing equipment from Renee," Shannon said.

"Okay," George said. "We should make plans at lunch."

Before they went upstairs, George reached into the box of books he had opened before. He quickly found *New York Underground* and put it under one arm.

Derrick's mom arrived, and he and Shannon left. George had ten minutes to shower and get to bed. Then, despite his exhaustion, he opened *New York Underground*.

The book was all about the secret world under New York City's streets. It was filled with diagrams showing how there was practically another city below the ground, a spaghetti mess of wires carrying telephone calls and electricity, pipes carrying water and sewage, and tunnels carrying trains. There were even old tubes that the post office had built to shoot tiny containers of mail across town. There were abandoned subway tunnels, long-buried basement rooms of old buildings, pockets of water. About ten years before, according to the book, a construction team not far from George's house had found an entire graveyard of slaves that had been built over.

Europeans had come to New York almost four hundred years ago. And before that the Manhattan Indians had lived there for thousands of years. Anything could be down there under the modern city.

George read until his eyes grew heavy and the book slipped from his fingers to the floor. He never heard his father come home.

But George didn't sleep well that night. In his dreams, he saw the door suddenly swing open below him and he fell, plunging into its dark mouth. As he neared the bottom, he woke up, sweating and gasping for breath.

He shivered and burrowed down into his covers. He and his friends still hadn't actually *seen* anything down there. Just a few glints from the water at the bottom. They didn't even know how much water was there. A puddle? A stream? A deep pool?

Lying there in the dark, George was glad they weren't going down until Saturday. He needed to get used to the idea of going underground, into the black unknown. He hoped Shannon was right, and the treasure was sitting right at the bottom of the hole.

But somehow he had a feeling that it was going to be more complicated than that.

Seven

Show-and-tell

When George got to their usual table at lunch the next day, he saw that Renee had joined Derrick and Shannon. She didn't look like a rock musician, the way Shannon did. Renee's hair was long and blonde, with no orange blotches, and she dressed kind of like an urban granola girl, in jeans, hiking boots, and polar fleece vests. George had always thought it was kind of weird that she and Shannon were friends.

"Hi, guys," George said, tucking his notebook under his lunch tray. He didn't want Renee asking him about the to-do list he'd made for the planning session.

Then he saw the unhappy scowl on Derrick's face. Derrick made eye contact with George, glanced sidelong at Renee, and nodded toward Shannon.

George glared at Shannon, who looked away quickly.

"You told her?" he asked in disbelief.

"Yeah, kind of."

George banged his hand on the table. "How could you do that?"

"I was asking her for some stuff for Saturday, and it kind of . . . slipped out," Shannon said.

"Slipped out?" Derrick said. "You just *accidentally* mentioned a three-hundred-year-old secret tunnel in George's basement?"

"Well, it was kind of suspicious, you know," Shannon argued. "I mean, borrowing all this rock-climbing equipment in the middle of Manhattan."

George covered his face with his hands. Here he was with the discovery of the century, and Shannon had blown it. If everyone else found out, there would be archaeologists and historians crawling all over his house. And *he* would never get anywhere near the basement again. The only place he'd get to see Captain Kidd's treasure would be in a museum.

"Anyway, we never said we wouldn't tell anyone," Shannon added.

George snorted. "I didn't think we had to!"

"Hey, guys!" Renee said. "Relax. I won't tell anyone. I just want to come along. It sounds totally cool."

"You can trust her. Okay?" Shannon pleaded.

"Well," George said, "it's not like we have much choice."

"Plus, I brought some cool stuff," Renee said. She

started rummaging around in her backpack. "My parents do spelunking in the Appalachian Mountains."

"Spelunking?" George asked.

"That's when you climb around in caves," Derrick supplied.

"And they have all kinds of equipment," Renee said. "Check out this thingy." She pulled out a little box with a tiny screen. It looked like a very small handheld computer.

"Watch this." Renee aimed the box at the ceiling, then pushed a button on the side. She peered at the screen. "The ceiling is twelve feet, eight inches from my hand."

George looked up at the high ceiling. It looked about twelve feet above his head. "That's pretty cool."

"I know," Renee said. "It's called a range finder. And it works in the dark."

"How does it work?" Derrick asked.

"It uses echoes, the same way submarines use sonar underwater."

"I didn't hear anything," George said.

"The sound is too high to hear," Renee said. "Like a dog whistle." She pointed the box at the far wall of the cafeteria. "Fifty-seven feet, three inches," she read. "You can tell exactly how deep a hole is or how far away a wall is."

Derrick leaned forward, his scowl gone. "Can I see that?"

Renee handed it to him. He started pinging things in the cafeteria.

"I can get ropes and harnesses, too. And climbing picks. And these." She pulled a couple of small walkie-talkies from her bag.

"I won't need one," Shannon said authoritatively. "I've got a cell phone."

"Your phone won't work underground," Renee said. "But these will. We can each carry one in case we get separated. You know, it can be pretty dangerous down there. You can run into pockets of poisonous gas, or cave-ins, or all kinds of things. It's important to stay in touch."

George remembered his nightmares about the hole and shivered. Maybe Shannon had been right to tell Renee. He didn't like it that another person knew about the secret door. But at least she knew what she was doing.

"And check this out." Renee reached into her backpack and pulled out a helmet, which she put on her head. On the front was a big light.

"What on earth is that?" Shannon said, laughing. "You look like a dork!"

"It's called a miner's helmet. So you can see in the dark." Renee flipped a switch on one side.

"Ow!" George said. The light was blinding.

"Turn it off!" Shannon cried.

The light went off, and George blinked. He tried to look around the cafeteria to see how many people had noticed. But all he could see was a big blue spot above his nose.

"Uh, I thought this was supposed to be a *secret* meeting," Derrick said.

"*Renee,*" Shannon complained. "We have to keep cool about this."

"I told my other friends I was doing a show-and-tell today," she said, shrugging. "About spelunking."

"Look, we all have to be careful," George said. "This could be the biggest buried treasure anyone has ever discovered. Don't tell *anyone* else. And don't talk about it where anyone can hear, okay?"

"Okay," Renee said.

"You either," he added to Shannon. "Not your parents, the lunch ladies, or your cat."

"I don't have a cat," she retorted. "But I swear I won't."

"Fine. Then let's just do a new pirate oath right now." George spat into his hand and held it out. "You too, Renee."

"Oh, no," Derrick said, looking around to make sure no one was watching. "Not another spit sandwich."

Eight

DOWN

It seemed like the week would drag on forever. But when Saturday finally arrived, George had mixed feelings about going underground. He'd had the falling nightmare twice the night before, and he woke up with a hollow feeling in his gut. It felt like he was facing a math test multiplied by a dentist's appointment. It didn't help that he kept remembering what Renee had said about poisonous gas and cave-ins. He was starting to feel that this whole adventure was pretty risky.

But then he thought about how it wasn't an ordinary adventure. It was an all-out quest. A chance to follow in Captain Kidd's footsteps and find Captain Kidd's treasure. And he couldn't wait to get down there.

That afternoon, Peter van Gelder was going out to a furniture store in New Jersey to buy bookshelves.

"Are you sure you don't want to come along?" he asked George.

"Um, how long do you think it'll take?" George asked.

"Three hours."

"Sounds good," George said. "Um—I mean, no, I can't. Derrick, Shannon, and Renee are coming over later. If that's okay," he added quickly.

"Oh, all right. Don't be too loud. Mr. and Mrs. St. John thought your party was a bit noisy."

"We're not having a party," George said, a little offended.

"So what are you doing?" his father asked.

"Uh, I don't know. Playing cards or something."

George hated lying to his father. As soon as he and his friends found Kidd's treasure, he would tell him everything. And his father could buy all the bookshelves in the world with the riches they found.

Peter van Gelder headed out the door. "There's still some birthday cake, if you and your friends want a snack. Call the St. Johns if you need anything."

"Okay. Bye, Dad."

The moment his father was out the door, George dialed Shannon's cell-phone number. She, Derrick, and Renee were waiting around the corner from George's house.

Shannon didn't even say hello. Just, "He's gone?"

George winced. "Give him time to get down the block."

"It's okay. We have a visual," she said.

"You've got a what?"

"We can see your dad. Don't worry, though. He won't see us."

Shannon hung up, and George went to the fridge. The mention of birthday cake had given him a good idea. He found four bottles of water. He knew the human body could go for weeks without food, but without water, you could die in a day or two.

George shivered. What was he thinking? They were only going to be down there for an hour or so. Climb down. Get treasure. Climb up. With luck the whole thing would only take thirty minutes.

Or maybe it was just an empty hole.

But what if it wasn't a hole at all? If the tunnels underneath the city were as complicated as *New York Underground* suggested, the hole could lead anywhere. In fact, Captain Kidd might not have built the secret door for a place to store treasure. The passage might have been a way for him to escape—a way to get out of his house if his enemies came to get him.

The doorbell rang. Derrick, Shannon, and Renee tromped in with three bulging backpacks. Renee was wearing her miner's helmet already. The packs clanked as they dropped heavily to the floor.

"Do you think you brought enough stuff, guys?" George asked.

"It pays to be prepared," Renee answered.

"Okay, but let's unpack down in the basement. Sometimes Mrs. St. John comes over and drops off a casserole or some cookies or something."

"She just comes in and leaves a casserole?" Shannon asked as the four of them clanked downstairs.

"She likes to look after us," George explained, switching on the light. "I think she just likes to take care of people."

"I don't see any secret door," Renee said as they stepped into the basement.

"That's because it's a secret." Shannon went to the stack of boxes by the wall. "Give me a hand."

The two girls pushed the boxes aside while George helped Derrick unpack. Renee had brought all the equipment she had promised and more. There were ropes and picks, hammers and spikes, helmets, harnesses, and gloves to wear.

"Are we planning to climb some subterranean mountain?" George asked.

"Like I said, it pays to be prepared," Renee explained. "You never know when you might have to go down a steep slope or . . . whoa."

She had just caught sight of the hole in the wall. She flicked on her helmet light and stuck her head into the hole.

"See?" Shannon said. "Secret door."

"Wow!" Renee let out a low whistle. "It was just behind the boxes?"

"Yeah. Wait until we open it," Shannon said. "And turn that light off! You're blinding me."

As soon as they opened the trapdoor, Renee pulled the range finder from a pocket. She pointed it down the hole, then checked the reading. "Forty-two feet, three inches," she said. "Not too bad."

She fitted them all with harnesses. "These will be attached to the rope. You can slide, but not too fast. So even if you let go of the rope, you won't fall."

"Cool," George said. The straps of the harness wrapped around his legs and back and over his shoulders. The thought that he couldn't really fall calmed his stomach a little.

Renee gave them each a few tools, which fit into the belt of the harness: a small hammer, a length of rope, and a walkie-talkie. They put on their climbing gloves, and George handed everyone a water bottle.

"I've only got three miner's helmets," Renee said. "Someone has to use a flashlight."

"I will," Derrick said quickly.

"Me," Shannon said at the same time.

"I'll take a flashlight," George blurted.

"What?" Renee said. "Don't you guys want helmets?"

Shannon giggled. "It's just that you look kind of . . . funny with that light on your forehead."

Renee pursed her lips. "It's not a fashion show down there. You'll wish you had one later," she said, digging out three flashlights.

George scooted through the opening and pointed his flashlight down the hole. In its powerful beam, he could see the entire hole. The walls were rough stone, and the water at the bottom looked still and shallow. He hoped.

Renee tossed a rope over a beam in the ceiling and expertly tied a knot.

"This rope will hold four hundred pounds, but we should go one at a time, just to be safe. I have to stay up here to fit the harnesses, so I'll go last. Who wants to go first?"

George took a deep breath. Part of him wished someone else would go first and make sure there were no half-buried corpses or deadly booby traps down there. But a bigger part of him wanted to be the first to explore Kidd's tunnel.

"I will," he and Shannon said at the same instant. They stared at each other.

"I'll be faster!" she insisted.

"No," George said quietly. "I have to do this."

She looked at him, then at the others. "All right. It's your house and everything."

"Thanks," George said.

Derrick peered down the hole again and whistled. "You guys are brave."

"I'm not brave," George admitted. "It's just that if something goes wrong, I want it to happen to me. So I won't have to face my dad."

No one laughed at the joke. Renee threaded the rope through the loops in his harness. "Use your feet against the wall. Go *slow.*"

George took a deep breath and went through the opening in the wall. He waited on the edge of the hole for a moment, wondering if he should back out and let Shannon go first.

"No way," he whispered to himself. He'd wondered about Kidd his whole life. Now he'd finally find out the truth.

George lowered himself into the hole.

The blackness swallowed him. He spun around on the end of the rope for a moment, his sense of direction completely lost. He felt like he was tumbling downward.

Instinctively, he thrust out his feet and bounced to a stop against the wall.

"I'm okay," he whispered. "All under control."

His hands grasped fiercely at the rope. He had to command himself to let go a little—he couldn't move unless he loosened his grip. The rope slipped in his hands, and he started to slide downward.

Once he was moving, it was easier. It was kind of like walking backward, only it was *down*ward. He let himself slide a few feet at a time and kept his feet solidly against the rough stone. Once he bounced too far off the wall, and his head banged against the other side of the tunnel.

"Ouch!" he muttered. Maybe he *should* have worn the helmet.

"You okay?" Renee called. Above him, the secret door was a little square of light.

"Yeah." His own voice echoed eerily.

After a few more minutes, George heard the sound of water behind him. He twisted and kicked to get his feet below him, and they touched the ground with a splash. Water slopped over the tops of his sneakers. It was only a few inches deep, but it was ice-cold. It sent a chill up his spine.

"I'm down!" he called.

"Okay," he heard Shannon say. "I'm next."

George pulled the rope from his harness. Standing on solid ground felt wonderful. He pulled the flashlight from his harness belt and switched it on.

"Whoa," he whispered, breathing in stale air as he looked around the tunnel.

Water ran down the middle, a shallow, slow-moving stream only about two feet wide. The ceiling was just high enough for him to stand up. He couldn't see very far in either direction.

George swept his flashlight across the ground. No sign of any treasure. There was just an old, moldy-looking log sitting in the middle of the stream. And the rocky walls and floor of the tunnel looked solid. You couldn't bury anything in them without dynamite.

He heard Shannon scuffling down behind him. She lowered herself into view, breathing hard.

"What a ride!" she said as her feet reached the ground.

George helped Shannon unclip her harness from the rope, and they called for Derrick to follow. From below, it sounded like he was having a hard time. He yelled about bumping his head once or twice, and when he finally arrived, he was hanging almost upside down. It took both of them to get him on his feet. Renee made the trip in less than thirty seconds, the rope whirring as she zoomed down.

"See, I said you should wear a helmet," she told Derrick, who was rubbing his head.

The four kids shone their lights around, filling the tunnel with dancing shadows.

"This is some cellar, George," Derrick said.

Shannon nodded. "I wish my house had one of these."

"I didn't think it would be so far down," Renee said. "It's going to be fun going back up."

George swallowed. He hadn't thought about climbing back out of the hole. What if he wasn't strong enough? What if none of them were able to climb out? He suddenly felt like the weight of the city overhead was crushing him. What if someone came into his basement and shut the secret door? And then sealed it over with concrete?

He shook his head. Thoughts like that would drive him crazy. Once the four of them were organized and moving, he'd stop panicking.

"Okay," he said. "Which way do we go?"

Derrick pulled out the map and pointed his flashlight at it.

"Well," he said, "I guess we're in this tunnel with the wavy line."

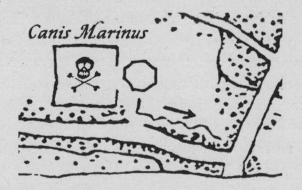

Canis Marinus

"But there's only one wavy line. We've got two choices. This way." Shannon pointed her flashlight up the tunnel. "Or that way." She pointed it in the other direction.

George furrowed his brow. The thought of false maps came to him. Pirates sometimes created fakes to lead their enemies into danger.

"We just have to figure out which way is which," Renee said. "The wavy line goes toward the bottom of the page."

George looked at the map and frowned. "I'm not sure what that means," he said. He swept his flashlight around the tight space. "In this direction the tunnel slopes down a little. . . . You think it means we should go that way?"

"Well, this arrow points the way we're supposed to go," Derrick said. He tapped his finger on a little arrow by the wavy line. "Maybe it's also pointing the direction that the water's flowing."

"So we're supposed to go downstream?" Shannon asked.

"Going downstream makes sense," George said. "If you were a pirate burying your treasure, you'd want it as deep as possible, right? And water flows down."

Shannon nodded. Derrick shrugged. Renee flipped on her blinding headlamp.

"So let's go down," she said.

*　　*　　*

Walking wasn't easy. The ground was covered with slimy rocks hidden by the water. The tunnel wasn't wide. They could touch both sides to steady themselves. Shannon was too tall to walk upright and had to hunch over. The rest of them also had to watch for outcroppings of rock above their heads. Renee wouldn't shut up about how great her helmet was. The second time George bumped his head, he started to wonder if she was right.

Their lights wavered along the walls, shadows flickering around them like crazy ghosts. Everything seemed to be in motion all the time down here. It made George dizzy.

The harnesses and equipment got heavier as they walked.

"Can't we leave this stuff here?" Derrick complained. "And get it on the way back?"

"What if we have to climb down another hole?" Renee asked.

"I sure wouldn't want to miss that," Derrick muttered, rubbing his head.

The slope got steeper, taking them farther and farther downhill. It was chilly and damp here. It felt like a movie theater in the middle of summer. After twenty minutes of slow progress, they reached a place where the tunnel split. George came to a halt.

"Map?" he asked Derrick.

Derrick pulled it out, and the other three crowded around him.

The tunnel they had been following appeared to lead to a three-way fork on the map, but the tunnel didn't match. They could go left or right, but not forward.

"How come there are only two paths here, but the map shows three?" George said.

They looked around, trying to find the missing tunnel.

"Maybe one of them got sealed up," Renee said.

"What do you think that is?" Derrick pointed at the map.

George looked over Derrick's shoulder. At the place where the tunnel split was a picture of an eye.

"Who knows?" George said. "Look, there's another eye, too. Maybe the eyes are clues."

"Maybe an eye means *look*," Shannon said.

"Yeah, or *look out*," Derrick suggested.

"Let's take a look around," George said. "See if we can figure out which tunnel to take."

The four turned their lights outward. George noticed that the walls weren't so solid here. There were cracks and seams. He pointed his flashlight into one, straining to see if anything could be hidden inside. One of the cracks was big enough for his hand. He gingerly stuck a finger in. The rock felt cold and slimy.

Suddenly, he felt a rumbling in the wall. His heart lurched. "Uh-oh!" He tried to snatch his hand away, but it felt stuck. He looked all around, trying to figure out what was happening. *It's a booby trap*, he thought. *I triggered it.*

"What is it?" Shannon demanded.

The sound built up all around them, shaking the floor under their feet, growing into an earthquake. The water danced in the stream, and it felt like the whole tunnel was about to collapse. George pointed his flashlight wildly down the different tunnels, trying to see what was coming at them.

Suddenly, the sound was right above them, as loud as a jet plane flying right overhead, about to break through the ceiling.

Then, slowly, the rumble died away, leaving them half deaf.

"What was *that*?" Derrick shouted.

George's ears rang, but he had suddenly remembered being fearful of dragons in the basement when he was little. He gave a shaky laugh and wiggled his finger out of the wall. "It was the subway."

"The subway? But that noise was—"

"Above us," George said. "We're *under* the subway tunnels."

"Phew!" Renee said. "I thought it was an earth-quake."

"I thought it was a booby trap," George admitted. "I'd just stuck my hand into the wall when it started. I thought I'd set something off."

"A booby trap?" Shannon asked.

"Um, yeah." George swallowed. "Pirates sometimes used to set traps to guard their treasure. You know, to kill people who tried to steal it."

"Booby traps? To *kill* people? Way to warn us, George," Derrick said.

"Well, I didn't want to scare you guys. I mean, Captain Kidd was a *privateer,* not a pirate. And it wasn't a trap, okay?"

"I bet this was, though," Renee broke in. "Look!"

The three followed the glare of her headlamp upward. Above their heads was an old, rusted metal grate. It was propping up a load of large rocks, enough to smash someone to bits.

"A trap?" George asked. "But how would it work?"

"Maybe it had to do with this," Shannon said. She reached out and grasped a long piece of rotted leather that hung down the wall. It was tied to the grate. "It could have been a kind of trip wire."

"Uh, Shannon, maybe you should let that go," Derrick said quickly.

"Come on, it's, like, three hundred years old. It can't work anymore." Shannon gave the leather strap a sturdy yank. It snapped off in her hand. "See?"

Suddenly, a metallic click came from the grate over their heads. No one said a word until another *click* sounded.

"Run!" George cried.

He bolted backward up the stream, splashing wildly until he fell sprawling into the shallow water. He could see the others scrambling down the two branching tunnels. Ominous creaking sounds came from the grate.

Then there was the shriek of grinding metal, and rocks tumbled from the tunnel ceiling. Dust engulfed his senses. He closed his eyes and threw up his arms to shield his head, flinching with each rumble of rolling boulders.

George lay on the ground, gagging from the grit in his mouth. When he could finally breathe again, he realized it was over. He opened his eyes, blinking away tears and dust.

A few feet away, he caught sight of a glimmer. He reached out and discovered it was his flashlight, submerged in the stream.

"Thanks, Renee," he said raggedly. Trust her to bring waterproof lights!

But where *was* Renee? Or Shannon or Derrick,

for that matter? Had he warned them in time?

George turned the flashlight toward the pile of rocks that the trap had dumped into the tunnel. The beam cut through the dust like a searchlight. He swallowed. A few big rocks had fallen only inches from him. The sight made him even more anxious for his friends.

George stood shakily. "Hello?" he called.

He heard a choked reply, but it disintegrated into coughing.

"Derrick?"

"Yeah," Derrick croaked. "Over here."

Derrick was on the other side of the pile of rocks, in the left fork of the tunnel, as near as George could tell. The rocks reached almost to the ceiling of the tunnel, but Derrick's flashlight flickered through the gap between the rocks and the ceiling.

"Are you okay?" George called.

"Yeah, but I fell into the stream. I'm soaked. So is the map."

"Can you remember it?" George asked hopefully.

"I think so, and part of the map is still dry."

"Good. Shannon? Renee?"

"I'm here," came Renee's voice. She sounded like she was in the other branch of the tunnel. "I'm fine. But a huge rock bounced right off my head. It's lucky I was—"

"Wearing your helmet," George and Derrick chimed in.

"So where's Shannon?" she said. "Shannon?"

The three of them were quiet for a moment, listening intently for an answer. Then they heard a small groan.

"Shannon?" Renee yelled.

"Okay," George said. "Everyone look around!"

He swept his flashlight across the edge of the rocks, hoping not to see an arm or leg sticking out from the pile.

Then he heard another groan behind him. He spun around and saw her.

Shannon lay facedown in the stream farther up the tunnel. She lifted her upper body and blinked in the glare of the flashlight, a dazed look on her face.

"Shannon?"

She nodded and growled, "Point that thing somewhere else."

A wave of relief flowed over George. "I found her!" he called to the others. "She's okay!"

Shannon pulled herself out of the water, groaning. She rubbed her head. "Next time, I'm wearing two helmets."

The four of them climbed carefully up the rock pile, meeting at the tiny air space at the top. They could just see one another's faces through the gap.

"Well, that Captain Kidd makes a mean trap," Derrick said. "We were lucky."

"That's true. If it hadn't been so old and rusty, it would have killed us all," George added. "We'll have to watch out. Next time, Captain Kidd might be the lucky one."

"It was a good try, though, Shannon," Renee said with a laugh.

"Yeah, way to almost get us all killed," Derrick added.

Shannon rubbed her head. "Just doing my part." Then she looked upward with a funny expression on her face. "Hey, check this out. Look up above."

They all shone their flashlights up to the roof of the tunnel, where the rocks had come from. But the tunnel didn't have a roof there. The beams sliced into the still-dusty air, seeming to go up forever.

"It's the third tunnel on the map," George gasped. "It goes *up*."

Nine

UP

It took them about twenty minutes to clear an opening large enough to get through. The third tunnel sloped up diagonally. It was about as steep as the bleachers in the school gym.

"We won't need rope to climb this," Renee said. "But watch your footing."

"That was pretty clever," Shannon said. "The tunnel is filled with rocks, and you can't get up to it unless you trigger the trap. It's like instant stairs."

"Or instant death," Derrick pointed out.

"Yeah, yeah," Shannon muttered. "Look, I'm sorry, all right?"

"So, I guess those eye symbols on the map do mean booby traps. Were there any other ones in this tunnel, Derrick?" George asked. He didn't want to run into any more of Captain Kidd's traps unexpectedly.

Derrick looked up at the ceiling, scanning his memory of the map. "Yeah. Our *privateer* friend was really guarding this tunnel. About halfway up there, there's an eye."

"Great," George said. "Then we shouldn't go this way."

"But it leads to the X," Derrick reminded him.

The four were silent for moment, all thinking the same thing. X *marks the spot!*

"Okay, I guess we've got to risk it, then. Just keep an eye out, everyone," George said.

"You bet we will," Renee agreed.

They crawled up the slope, moving carefully. Shannon stayed in front, and no one argued with her. George was amazed that she could move with such confidence after the booby trap had almost crushed them all.

He scanned his flashlight across the steep slope constantly, checking the rocky tunnel floor before every step. He wondered what other sorts of traps Kidd might have created and if they would still work after three centuries.

He swallowed. It would be weird to be killed by a trap that was set by a man who had died three centuries ago. Maybe Derrick was right, and Kidd really had been a pirate. These booby traps made him seem a lot more criminal, like he had something to hide.

Of course, George reflected, he probably had a lot of enemies.

At least the four of them had the map—or

Derrick's memory of it—to help them try to avoid a sudden, horrible end.

George checked his watch. An hour and a half had gone by. Half the time before his father would be coming home. They'd have to turn around soon.

The climbing seemed to take forever. In the first tunnel, the stream had smoothed out the gentle slope over the centuries. But here the way was studded with jagged rocks. The tunnel was growing tighter, too, until they had to crawl in single file.

Finally, they reached a narrow hole, barely big enough to squeeze through. Shannon came to a halt.

"Do you think you can fit, Shannon?"

"Yeah, I can fit. But I'm not sure I want to."

"Huh?"

"Well, if I were going to put a trap somewhere in this tunnel, I'd put it right here."

George nodded. He was glad to see Shannon wasn't insanely brave. Anyone who crawled into that small hole would be taking a risk. They could easily trip a wire and not know it. The slightest shift in the rocks could crush them.

He looked at his watch again. "Maybe we should turn around."

"No way," Shannon said. "It took us forever to get here."

"Exactly. My dad will be home in an hour and

ten minutes."

"I just want to test this with something." Shannon unwound some rope from her belt and threw it through the hole. She pulled it back.

Nothing happened.

"You weigh a lot more than a piece of rope, Shannon," Derrick pointed out.

"Maybe. But I don't want to just go home now. We could be really close to the treasure."

Shannon and Derrick continued to argue. George realized that he should make the call. It was *his* dad who was coming home. He'd be the one in trouble if they were caught. Well, the *most* trouble, anyway.

He checked his watch again. It had taken them almost two hours to get here. But it should be a lot quicker on the way back. They wouldn't have to dig or worry about traps. On the other hand, they had to face the climb back up to the secret door.

"Be quiet, guys," he interrupted. "We have to turn around."

Shannon opened her mouth, but she didn't say anything for a moment. When she did speak, it was in a whisper.

"Do you hear that?"

They all listened. Coming through the narrow

passage was a noise. It sounded almost like people talking.

George crept up to the hole. A soft, warm wind was coming through.

"Maybe this goes up to the surface," he said.

"Let's try it, then," Shannon said. "You might get home quicker this way."

George listened again. The voices sounded angry, threatening. He swallowed. Something was going on up there. Something unpleasant.

Then he heard another voice. This one sounded scared.

George sighed. They couldn't just turn around now.

"Okay," he said. "We're going on."

Not waiting for an answer, he pulled himself up through the hole. His eyes scanned for any sign of a trap. He imagined the hole closing in on him, the jagged rocks like teeth cutting him in half.

But then he was through. Nothing had happened.

"It's okay," he whispered. "Come on. But everyone stay quiet. We are officially sneaking now."

The other three pulled themselves through the passage. The tunnel on this side was even more narrow. George stayed in front, looking for traps and listening as the sounds grew closer. There were at least two people. He could hear them plainly now. One spoke in low and threatening tones. The other sounded like a kid—a kid trying to hide the fear in his voice.

The tunnel grew wider and the air warmer. Maybe they really were headed toward the surface, and they were just overhearing an argument in a basement apartment. But the voices had an echoing quality, as if they were in a large cavern.

Suddenly, the way was blocked by another pile of rocks. The voices were very close.

George turned back to the others and pointed at one of his eyes. The other three nodded. This must have been one of the traps indicated by eye symbols on the map. George thought somebody must have set it off a long time ago, or maybe not so long.

He turned off his flashlight and gestured for the other three to do the same. But when the last light went off, it wasn't completely black. A shaft of light came through a hole above the pile. Just like the last time, an overhead tunnel had been opened when the rocks fell.

George climbed upward, careful not to make a sound. He wondered who had been unlucky enough to spring the trap and if there was a body under the pile.

The voices sounded like they were just on the other side of the rocks.

"Just tell us where it is," a man said.

"Forget it," a boy answered.

"You'll tell us sooner or later."

"That's what you think."

George carefully climbed a few more feet. His head was just below the opening now. He peeked upward.

The glow from above wasn't sunlight. It was a bright, artificial light, like the big lights George had seen construction teams use when they worked at night. As his head cleared the edge of the passage, he squinted in the sudden glare.

The tunnel above him had a rounded ceiling, decorated with crumbling old tiles. There were two raised platforms about five feet high running down either side. Metal beams braced the tunnel, and the harsh light showed lettering stenciled on the side of one:

PROPERTY OF MTA

George's eyes widened. The MTA was the Metropolitan Transportation Authority. This was a subway station. But it was too broken down to be in use. It must be abandoned.

George had read about the old stations in the *New York Underground* book. It had mentioned that the MTA stored equipment in a few, and in the completely abandoned ones, homeless people sometimes built underground shelters.

George turned his head and found the source of the voices. He ducked down, trying to stay out of sight.

Three big men were huddled around a smaller person. One of them was the man doing the yelling. The smaller person was sitting on a chair—*tied* to the chair, George realized with a flicker of horror.

It was a boy about his age. The boy was incredibly dirty, his hair greasy and matted. Under the grime, his face was set in a defiant expression.

"Think you can hold out forever? You'll get hungry sooner or later. Then you'll tell us."

"I don't get hungry," the boy said.

"Well, if you don't, I bet the rats will. They're crawling all over the place."

The men laughed, but George knew there was nothing funny about them. These guys meant business.

The thought of rats also made him queasy. Waiting for the subway, he had often seen them scurrying down on the tracks. It was easy to ignore them when you were up on the platform. But here he was *under* the subway.

Suddenly, George caught motion out of the corner of his eye. *No,* he thought, *there's no way.*

He turned his head and found himself face-to-face with a big gray subway rat, only a few inches away. Its black eyes glittered at him.

George uttered a strangled cry and lost his footing. He slipped, rolling down the rock pile. As he hit the bottom, his ankle exploded in pain.

"Are you okay?" Derrick asked, turning on his flashlight.

"Shhh!" George hissed, waving the light away. Derrick switched it off, and George was blind in the sudden darkness.

"What was that?" a man's voice said from above.

"Check it out." That was the threatening voice of the one who'd been questioning the boy.

Crunching footsteps came toward the hole. George heard the sound and recognized it—gravel. Some of the subway tunnels were floored with gravel.

A beam of light sprang on, probing through the hole. Renee, Derrick, and Shannon shrank back into the shadows as the beam searched. George tried to move from the edge of the pile carefully, and his ankle throbbed with pain. The light was getting closer, and he could see the outline of a face looking down into the hole.

He tried to lift himself slowly from the rocks without disturbing any. It was like a huge game of pick-up sticks.

Unfortunately, George wasn't very good at pick-up sticks.

One of the rocks under him slipped, rolling down the pile with a clatter. The beam of light instantly found him.

"Hey, it's a kid!"

"Run!" George cried.

He took a few steps, but pain shot through his ankle again. He crumpled to the ground, his knees banging onto the hard, rocky floor of the tunnel. His three friends were moving quickly, their flashlights dancing away.

At the top of the rock pile, the man was grunting as he tried to squeeze through the passage. Just his feet and legs were showing.

George knew he had to think fast. Once the man was through, he'd be defenseless. He picked up a big rock and heaved it up at the guy.

"Ow!" came a yell. The man dropped his flashlight, which bounded down the rock pile, and pulled himself back up and out of sight. "Little creep threw a rock at me!"

"Get out of my way," came the other voice. Two big boots came through the hole now. They kicked aside the topmost rocks, clearing a bigger space.

George stood up gingerly and grabbed another rock to throw. How long could he fend them off?

A hand closed on his wrist.

He spun around and realized it was Shannon.

"Come on," she whispered. She put one shoulder under his arm. Her support kept George's weight off his injured ankle, and she pulled him down the tunnel at a jog.

Derrick and Renee had come back, too. They held their flashlights down at the ground so that George and Shannon could see. George's ankle hurt every time he stepped on it, but he gritted his teeth and said, "I can go faster."

They went faster.

"Come back here!" A shout came from behind them. One of the men had made it down the rock pile. George dared a look backward.

A bobbing flashlight showed that someone was chasing them. He wasn't moving as fast as the four kids, though. The flashlight beam was probing the walls warily. He must have known about the booby traps.

They reached the narrow passage. Derrick and Renee squeezed through.

"Can you make it?" Shannon said.

"Sure, but you first. You'll be faster."

"No way. Go on!"

George dropped gingerly to his knees and pulled himself through the hole. The rocks tore at his shirt and banged his injured ankle. He froze for a moment, paralyzed by the pain.

"You okay?"

George wasn't okay. His ankle throbbed, and he just wanted to rest. But he knew that if he stopped now, Shannon would be trapped on the other side with their pursuer.

Taking a deep breath, he pulled himself through the hole. He slid a few more feet down the steep, rocky slope. Shannon scrambled through after him.

"I don't think I can go on any farther," he said.

"What do we do?" Derrick asked. He and Renee had waited for them.

"Come on, just a little bit farther," Shannon said. "I've got a plan."

She pulled George up, and they made it a few more yards down the tunnel. Every step was agony, but George just shut his eyes and let Shannon lead him. They hadn't gotten very far when Shannon stopped and let George sink to the floor.

"I'll be back," she said.

He opened his eyes to see that Shannon had turned around. Shannon was headed back to the narrow passage. What was she doing?

After ten seconds or so, Shannon came back and whispered, "Shhh. I left them a present."

They all turned off their flashlights and waited in darkness.

A few minutes later, two voices approached. Light flickered through the narrow hole.

"They must have gone through here."

"They're miles ahead of us. Clever little sewer rats."

"Not the one I saw. He looked like a topside kid. He had regular clothes. Even climbing gear."

"Still, we'll never catch them."

"He was limping. Go on through."

"Are you kidding? Look at that hole! Could be one of Kidd's traps. I stick to the subway tunnels."

The other voice sighed. "All right, I'll go, then."

A flashlight stabbed straight through the hole, and a head appeared.

George stiffened, ready to try and run again. His ankle felt a bit better now. Maybe they could make it. . . .

But Shannon held him down.

The man crept through slowly, shining his flashlight carefully around the edge of the passage. Then suddenly, the beam stopped moving.

George could see it now. The man had found what Shannon had left at the hole. He could see that it was the piece of rotting leather she had pulled from the trap in the main tunnel.

"Oh, no!" the man said, pulling himself back out of the passage.

"What happened?"

"You were right. It is a trap. Wonder how he got through it."

"Maybe it doesn't work anymore."

"You want to try it?"

"It's not worth it. Forget him. He was just a kid. Let's get back to the boy."

"Do you think he really knows where it is?"

"We know he found it. He's just hidden it somewhere. He'll talk sooner or later."

Two sets of footsteps scrambled away, the dancing lights through the hole fading to blackness. Finally, there was no more sound. George sighed with relief.

"That was pretty devious, Shannon," he said. "Thanks."

"Yeah, great idea!" Renee agreed.

"You're a regular pirate!" Derrick said, grinning at her.

Shannon laughed. "That's *privateer* to you, Derrick."

One by one, they flicked their lights back on. They stared at one another in shock. All four of them were covered with dirt. Their clothes were ripped, and sweat made the grime run in black lines down their faces.

"You guys look awful," Derrick said.

"You should see yourself," Shannon retorted.

"So, what was up with those men?" Renee asked. "Why were they chasing us?"

"Good question." George hadn't read anything in *New York Underground* that explained what he'd seen in the subway tunnel. "They were holding some kid prisoner."

"Really?" Shannon exclaimed. "You think they snatch kids off the street and bring them down here? They kidnap them for ransom?"

"I don't think so," Derrick said. "I bet they're looking for the treasure, too."

"Why do you think that?" Renee asked.

"They know about Captain Kidd's traps."

Derrick was right, George realized, dismayed. They were all down here for the same reason. One of the men had said the name *Kidd*. Or had they just meant *a* kid?

His mind was filled with questions. Who else knew about the treasure? How had the men found their way here without a map? How long had they been looking? How many secret doors to the tunnels were there?

George shook his head. This was all too complicated to think about now. "Let's get out of here," he said.

"How's your ankle?" Renee asked.

George tested his weight carefully. "It's a little better. I think I can walk now. But no more running."

"How much time do we have before your dad gets home?" Derrick asked.

George looked at his watch and gulped. "Forty minutes."

"No running, huh?" Shannon said. "Think we can make it in time?"

Gritting his teeth, George hobbled down the tunnel. "Let's just hope my dad's late."

Ten

"LEAVE NO ONE BEHIND"

By the time they made it back to the dangling rope, George's ankle was throbbing again.

"How much time left?" Renee asked.

"Twenty minutes," George answered. They'd made it back surprisingly quickly. You could move a lot faster down a tunnel when you knew where you were going.

"Where's your dad again?" Derrick asked.

"Buying bookshelves at a big store out in New Jersey."

"It's not like that would take *exactly* three hours, George. He was just guessing."

"You don't know my dad." Peter van Gelder planned everything down to the minute.

George looked up at the small square of light above his head and wondered how he would ever make it up. Rope climbing wasn't his best skill even when both ankles were working fine.

"I can't do it," he said.

"Don't worry," Renee said. "I've got it all figured out. You go first, Shannon."

Shannon threaded her harness and scuttled upward. Derrick went up easily, too. Then Renee clipped the rope to her own harness.

"I'm going last?" George said. "You're just going to leave me down here?"

"Yep. That way, if you can't make it, we can pull you up."

Renee shimmied up the rope, leaving George all alone. When her headlamp disappeared through the door above, he was in almost total blackness. He looked down the tunnel, wondering if the two men had decided to follow them after all. Maybe they were sneaking up on him right now in the darkness.

He fumbled the rope into his harness and started to climb.

It wasn't so hard because he could rest between climbs. Wearing the harness, he didn't have to worry about holding up his own weight. It was actually easier than a rope climb in gym.

But with his injured ankle, George couldn't use his feet to help him. His arms were worn out in no time at all. Halfway up, he knew he wasn't going to make it. He strained for a few more yards but was still ten feet from the door when his arms refused to pull any farther. The harness kept him from slipping down, but he couldn't go up, either.

He tried not to imagine himself hanging there forever in the blackness.

"It's too hard," he shouted up.

"Okay," Renee called. "Just hold on."

He waited and heard the sounds of straining from above. The rope started to move upward. The three others were pulling him out.

George felt himself inching upward until the edge of the secret door drew within reach. Then he reached up with his aching arms and yanked himself through the opening.

"Whew!" Derrick gasped. "You sure weigh a lot for a skinny guy."

George leaned back against the cool basement wall with relief, eyes blinking in the light. "Thanks, guys. For everything—coming back to save me from those men, pulling me out of the hole."

"You don't have to thank us," Shannon said.

"Yeah," Derrick added. "We took an oath."

"Remember?" said Renee. "We don't leave anyone behind."

George smiled, remembering that line. He had added it right at the end, as an afterthought. He was glad he had now.

"Let's get this place cleaned up," Shannon

ordered. "Haul up the rope in case they're following us."

George gulped and quickly pulled up the dangling rope. The last thing he needed was those men finding their way into his basement.

He and Derrick closed the secret door and piled the equipment on top of it. Then Derrick and Shannon pushed the boxes back to cover up the hole in the wall. Renee pulled out a first-aid kit from her backpack and bound George's ankle with a bandage. She squeezed it in a few places, asking where it hurt.

"This doesn't seem too bad," she said. "You should be okay in a couple of days."

"Thanks. It feels much better with the bandage." George flexed his ankle. "You really know a lot of cool stuff, Renee."

"Thanks."

"I'm glad you're one of us."

Renee smiled.

George glanced at his watch. "All right, you guys," he announced. "You have five minutes to get out of here. Let's get together tomorrow at Shannon's house. We've got to plan what to do next."

The other three nodded soberly. The world below the city had proved a lot more complicated and dangerous than they'd ever imagined. But the four of them had successfully avoided all the traps and had even escaped being captured.

George wondered about the boy he'd seen in the subway tunnel. Where had he come from? What did those men want from him?

He glanced at his watch again as they climbed the stairs. Right on time. He opened the front door.

Uh-oh. His father's car was pulling up in front of the house.

"My dad!" he cried. He slammed the door, and the other three crashed into him from behind.

"We are so busted," Derrick moaned.

"What do we do, George?" Shannon asked.

George tried to think clearly. "Go out the back," he said. "Derrick, you know the way. Over the fence and into the back of that convenience store on Broadway."

"Right," Derrick called. "Come on, guys." The three ran toward the kitchen and the backyard. George stood on tiptoe and looked out of the front door's tiny window. His dad's hatchback was open, two long white boxes sticking out. Bookshelves. As he watched, Peter van Gelder honked the horn, the signal for George to come out and help him unload.

George waited, listening as his friends crashed through the kitchen. It sounded like they'd run into something. He pictured the contents of the fruit bowl rolling all over the kitchen floor. His father beeped again impatiently. Finally, the sound of the back door closing reached him.

George took a deep breath and headed out the front door.

Peter van Gelder was halfway up the steps. "Good, you can give me a hand with—" he began. Then he stopped and stared. "Good heavens, George. What happened to you?"

George looked down at himself. His clothes were torn and soiled, and his hands were almost black with dirt. He should have been cleaning up instead of just standing by the door like an idiot. But now it was too late.

He dusted himself off hurriedly. "I, uh, decided to clean the basement."

"You decided to *what*?"

"Well, uh, my friends left early, and I didn't have anything to do."

"And you decided to clean the basement?"

"Yeah. It was dirty. Really dirty."

His father blinked in amazement. "Well, that was very nice of you, George," he said with a hint of suspicion.

"That's okay."

"Need some help?" a voice called.

It was Mr. Roulain, coming up the street in a sweatshirt and jeans. George sighed with relief. With his twisted ankle, it would have been agony to carry anything. Mr. Roulain and George's father carried the boxes while George held the doors open.

"I see you're wearing the watch I gave you," Mr. Roulain said as he was leaving. "And getting dirty, too."

"Yeah," George said sheepishly. "I've been cleaning. But the watch has been really useful. Thanks again."

When George limped inside, his dad was looking down through the basement door. He turned. "Wow, you really did clean up." A worried look crossed his face. "I hope you didn't move all those heavy boxes. You don't need a bad back at your age."

"No, I didn't," George said. He was sort of telling the truth. He'd been having his ankle bandaged while Derrick and Shannon pushed the boxes back. The basement did look better. It was a good thing that he had an explanation for all the changes down there.

"That's just great," his father said. "You know that I've been keeping most of my books down there. And some of your mother's, too. I'm going to move them to my study once I get these shelves put together. This is a big help."

George nodded. He gave his dad a smile, but his head was spinning. He was glad to hear that his father didn't just want to hide away all reminders of his mother anymore. But he was also plotting ahead. If his father started emptying the boxes of books, he would uncover the hole in the basement wall.

And through that hole was the secret door.

The next day, the four of them met at Shannon's place. Like most people in New York City, Shannon lived in an apartment. It was full of funky stuff that her parents had collected when their band toured the world. The band had never been popular in the United States, but it seemed like they'd been famous in just about every other country.

One wall was covered with photographs of Shannon as a baby, on tour with her parents. On her shelves were all kinds of musical instruments that George didn't even recognize. Her computer was playing weird music from Nova Scotia or Iceland or someplace. They all sat in beanbag chairs, George holding a glass of ice water against his ankle.

On the floor in front of them was a New York subway map. George had spent the morning with his mother's book about the history of the subway system. He had marked the places where he thought they had gone.

"Okay," George started. "Problem number one: My dad is planning on moving all those boxes of books. When he does, he'll run straight into the secret door."

"How did he miss it till now?" Renee asked.

"It was buried under six inches of dirt," Derrick said. "Until we found it and dug it up last Tuesday."

"Well, it would be a pain to bury it again," George said. "I mean, if we ever want to use it."

"Which we definitely do," said Renee.

"Maybe we could cover up the door somehow," Shannon said. "With a piece of wood that we can move in and out or something."

"Do you think your dad even noticed that hole in the wall before?" Derrick asked.

"Probably not. Those books have been down there forever, and he never goes into the basement. He doesn't think about stuff like fixing the house."

"Well, that's lucky," Derrick said. "If he'd gotten the wall sealed up, we never would have found the door."

"So we have to do something that makes the

floor look solid," Shannon said. "But that we can open and close. How long do we have?"

"Until he puts those bookshelves together, which he's doing right now."

Shannon sat up. "That's major trouble, George. He could finish today. We need to go create a diversion or something."

"Relax." George pulled a small plastic bag from his pocket and dropped it on the floor. It was one of the packages of screws and braces that had come with the bookshelves. He'd snatched it this morning before his dad had gotten started. "I don't think he'll be finishing today."

"Oh, man, George, you're cold-blooded," Derrick said, laughing.

"That's problem number one solved for now," George said. "Now for problem number two."

He told them in detail about what he'd witnessed in the abandoned subway tunnel: the captive boy, the men, the threats.

"Wow," Derrick muttered. "I could hear people talking, but I had no idea this was going on."

"And the boy looked like he *lived* down there in the subway. His skin was covered with soot, like he hadn't had a bath in, like, months."

"He's in trouble," Shannon said. "We should help him."

They were all quiet for a moment.

"So what are we going to do?" Renee said.

"What *can* we do?" Derrick asked. "We don't know anything about what's going on down there. It's like a different planet or something."

"No, it's not," Renee said. "It's *this* planet. I've read about people who live down in the subways and tunnels. They're not aliens, they're just homeless people."

"Who live *underground*," Derrick said.

Shannon shook her head. "That's just because they don't have anyplace else to live. It's better than being out in the rain."

"I'm not saying we shouldn't help a homeless kid," Derrick argued. "The problem is, we don't know what's going on down there. We don't know who those guys are or what they want. It's not like this kid is someone at our school or something. He's someone who lives in an abandoned subway tunnel. Come on, guys. That's seriously weird."

"Yeah, it's weird," George said. "But so is collecting saltines."

"Hey!" Derrick protested. "That was a secret!"

"You collect *what*?" Shannon said.

George grinned. "He's got a big dresser drawer full of them. *Full.* He gets a few packets from the cafeteria every day and takes them home."

"Thanks a lot, George," Derrick said. "Yes, I collect saltines. But that doesn't exactly compare with living underground."

"I don't know, Derrick." Renee shook her head. "It's pretty weird. I mean, do you eat them? Or do you just, you know, save them?"

George hid a grin. Derrick was glowering. "Can we please drop this?"

"Anyway," Shannon said. "We *have* to go back and help that kid. We don't have a choice. We took an oath."

"That's right," Renee agreed.

Derrick scowled. "I don't remember anything in the oath about rescuing weird underground kids."

Shannon closed her eyes. "The last line was, 'And we will never leave anyone behind.'"

"I thought that just meant us," Derrick complained.

"The oath said *anyone*."

"George?"

They all looked at him. He started to shrug, but it had been *his* oath after all. And he was the one with the secret door in his basement. It seemed like whenever some uncomfortable question came up, he became the leader of the group.

"Um, well, I did kind of mean just us," he admitted.

"See?" Derrick said.

"But the oath actually said we wouldn't leave *anyone* behind," George went on. "And that kid *is* someone."

Derrick groaned.

"And the point of the oath was that we'd all trust each other," Shannon said, "down there in the dark."

"So?"

"So, if we don't bother to help someone who obviously needs help, how can we trust each other?"

George nodded. He remembered when he'd fallen from the rock pile and the man was coming through the hole. For a moment, he'd been alone there, unable to move. The other three could have just left him, but they'd risked themselves to pull him to safety. The thought that anyone would be left down there gave him the chills.

"All right, I'll go along. An oath's an oath," Derrick agreed. He shook his head. "But I can't believe you told them about the saltines."

"We're going to have to move fast," Renee said. "Who knows what those guys will do to him?"

George frowned. "Well, my dad's bridge night is Tuesday, just two days from now."

"That's too long," Shannon said flatly. "We have

to go tonight."

"Tonight?" Derrick cried.

"After George's dad goes to sleep."

"What about George's ankle?" Renee put in.

"How is it?" Shannon asked.

George flexed his foot. "It's better, I guess."

"Better enough to stumble around underground?" Derrick said. "To dodge falling rocks? To climb up and down ropes? *To run away from bad guys?*"

George blinked. His ankle still hurt when he walked, and the thought of running made him wince. But then he imagined the kid down in that old subway tunnel, tied to a chair with no hope of rescue. He swallowed.

"My ankle's fine."

"It's settled, then," Shannon said. "We go tonight. At midnight."

Eleven

Operation: Midnight

"Rope?"

"Check."

"First-aid kit?"

"Check."

"Walkie-talkies?"

"Check."

"Helmet lights?"

George, Shannon, and Derrick flicked on their miner's helmets, flooding George's basement with light. Renee had volunteered to use the flashlight this time, since she had the most experience spelunking.

"All right, we're ready!" Shannon exclaimed.

"Be quiet!" George gestured toward the ceiling nervously. His dad was fast asleep and three tall floors above, but he still wished everyone would remember to whisper.

The hard part had been waiting for midnight before creeping down from his room. He'd lain awake staring at the ceiling, his mother's locket clutched in one hand. In a strange way, George felt that by exploring Kidd's history, he was some-how getting closer to her. She had always loved to tell him stories about old New York, especially their house. George wished she were here to share in this discovery.

When he had made his way carefully to the bottom of the creaky stairs, he found the other three waiting as planned, right at the front door. They had all managed to sneak out of their apart-ments, too.

Now they were in the basement, ready to go. Their harnesses were on, the equipment all dis-tributed. The secret door was open and waiting.

"Okay, then," Shannon said. "Let's go."

This time, the descent into blackness didn't seem so bad. George's stomach had gotten used to the idea of sliding down the rope toward an invisible destination.

The four of them splashed down the little stream. They each carried a map—Derrick had redrawn one from memory and made copies for everyone. That way one lost or damaged map wouldn't cause a problem. And if they got sepa-rated, any of them could make it out on their own.

Of course, George thought, *the plan is* not *to get separated.*

They arrived at the rock pile in about ten minutes. It was much quicker now that they'd traveled the tunnels once before.

"Where do you think these other two tunnels go?" Renee asked.

"We can explore them some other time," Shannon said. "Right now, we should stick to the mission."

George looked at his map. It showed the other two tunnels, but one of them faded away—like the creator of the map just hadn't gotten around to finishing it—and the other ran off the bottom of the map, in the opposite direction from the X. It looked like Kidd hadn't buried his treasure in either of them. But it was amazing to think that whole other adventures might await down those two paths.

They climbed the rock pile up to the sloping tunnel.

"How's the ankle?" Derrick asked.

George shrugged. Climbing the steep, rocky surface had started a twinge of pain in his ankle, but he bit his lip. He didn't want the others worrying about him. However uncomfortable *he* was, the captive boy was having a much worse time. "I'm okay."

They got to the narrow passage, and the group fell silent. This was where the men had given up chasing them the last time. They might be anywhere around here now. And sound traveled in strange ways through the tunnels.

Shannon squeezed through first.

Halfway through, she stopped and whispered, "Check it out."

Her helmet light shone on a dark blotch on a rock. It reflected the light in a weird way.

"What is it?"

"Looks kind of like . . . blood."

"Blood?"

She looked back at George. "Yeah, you beaned that guy with a rock, remember?"

"Great," he said. "He must be really aching to get his hands on me now."

Shannon grimaced and slithered out of sight. The rest of them crept through the passage, avoiding the blotch of blood for good measure.

Now they moved more slowly, trying not to make any noise. There were a lot of loose rocks here, and George had to be extra careful not to set his foot on any. The last thing he needed was to turn his ankle again—or twist the other one.

Shannon stopped and raised her hand. They came to a halt.

She turned back toward them and said in the softest whisper, "Lights off."

One by one, they turned off the lights on their miner's helmets and Renee flicked off her flashlight, until the tunnel was plunged into total darkness.

Now we can't see anything, George thought. How were they supposed to find their way forward?

But after he'd stood a minute in the dark, his eyes adjusted. A light appeared ahead. It was coming from above, spilling down onto jagged shapes in the tunnel before them.

They had reached the pile of rocks that marked Kidd's second trap along this path. The more George's eyes adjusted to the darkness, the clearer everything became. At the top of the pile was the hole that led up to the abandoned subway station. A shaft of light was spilling down through it.

There were lights on up above. That probably meant the men were still around.

No noise came through the hole, though. As they stood there waiting for their eyes to adapt, all George could hear was a slow *drip, drip, drip* of water.

Shannon walked quietly up to the rock pile and slowly placed one foot on it. She shifted her weight onto the foot, reaching out with her hands.

George felt his jaw tighten. He was waiting for a rock to slip, for Shannon to fall. His stomach was jumpy again. He felt that if she made a single sound, he would launch himself into a dead run back down the tunnel. He steeled himself, silently repeating the oath they had taken: "We will never leave anyone behind."

Shannon climbed up the pile without making any noise. With one look back at the other three, she poked her head above the lip of the hole.

George swallowed. When he had spied on them, the men might not have known about the hole. But now they would probably be keeping an eye on it.

Shannon turned around slowly, scanning in all directions. Finally, she shrugged and pulled herself up and out of sight.

George, Derrick, and Renee all looked at one another. They hadn't really made a plan about how to rescue the boy or even how to find him. All they had decided was to come here first. But now that they were here, going farther seemed incredibly risky.

"I'll go next," Derrick whispered finally. He climbed up the pile and through the hole.

Renee followed, making it through without a sound.

George sighed. He tested his ankle, flexing it. The tender muscles felt okay, but he couldn't shake his nervous feeling. He could already imagine himself crashing down again, probably breaking his leg and making enough noise to wake up his father back on Windsor Lane.

One step at a time, he thought. Clenching his jaw, he began to climb.

By the time he reached the top, his legs were shaking with the effort. Sweat began to pour from underneath the helmet into his eyes. His ankle ached. But he had made it up without making any noise.

George blinked as he emerged into the subway station. The big construction lights were still set up, filling the station with a bright, cold glare. The other three kids seemed eerily illuminated as they spread out, exploring the cavernous space. George hadn't realized before how big it was, as wide as a house and as long as a street block.

Shannon looked at him and shrugged. "Looks like no one's here," she said. Her voice echoed eerily, bouncing off the concrete walls.

"Do you think they left because of us?" Renee asked.

"I don't think they're gone for good," Derrick said. He was up on the station platform. "They left their lights."

"They left their lights *on*," Shannon added. "They could come back at any moment."

George shivered, looking around.

Next to the lights was a bunch of electronic equipment—batteries, a radio, and some stuff that George didn't recognize. There were also pickaxes and climbing gear. These guys were ready for spelunking.

The walls were covered with graffiti, spray-painted pictures and words added since the station had been abandoned. Down one side in three-foot-high letters were the words:

LEROY MAKES THE RULES

Down the other side, George saw the name again.

LEROY SAYS GET OUT! STAY OUT!

"Who's Leroy?" he wondered aloud.

"I don't know," Derrick answered. "But I'd rather not meet him."

"Hey," Renee called. "Look at this."

She was at one end of the station, where the tunnel stretched off into blackness. The three of them joined her.

"It looks like a camping tent," George said.

The little tent was twenty feet or so down the tunnel, far enough that the light from the station hit only a corner of it. The tent sagged sadly, as if it had been rained on. But it never rained down here, a hundred feet underground. Did it?

"You think anyone's in there?" Derrick whispered.

Shannon took a breath and walked up to the tent. "Hello?"

There was no answer, so she grabbed one flap and peeked inside.

"Oh, that's awful," she said, flapping a hand in front of her nose. "No one's in there, but it sure smells bad."

"Look," Renee said. "There's more."

George looked deeper into the darkness, letting his eyes adjust again. He could see more structures in the gloom. Some were tents, but most were crude shelters. They were made of old boards and tattered sheets. A few broken chairs stood in a circle around a burned-out fire.

"Wow, this is like a shantytown," Renee said.

"A what?"

"When a group of homeless people make their own little neighborhood," she explained, "they live in shanties. Houses they build themselves."

"There must be twenty or thirty shelters here," George said. It was one thing to realize that one kid lived underground. But the thought of a whole community existing down here made his head spin. It made him feel bad for them, too, but at least they had one another.

"Yeah," Shannon said. "A lot of houses. But no people."

"Where do you suppose they all went?"

"Maybe things got better and they all found jobs or something," Derrick said.

"I doubt it." Renee reached down and picked up a frying pan. It was clean and in good repair. "Look at all this stuff they left behind. As if they had to leave in a hurry."

"Maybe Leroy forced them out," Shannon said.

"Or maybe Leroy's just some crazy guy with a can of spray paint," Derrick said, nerves creeping into his voice.

"Yeah, or maybe—"

"Shhh!" Renee hissed.

She was pointing back the way they had come. George froze, looking back into the station. He couldn't see anything. But he heard a far-off noise, and a trickle of sweat ran down his back.

Shannon turned to Renee and opened her hands wide in a gesture of confusion. Renee gestured with her flashlight, as if she were beaming it around.

George looked again. Peering through the station and into the darkness of the tunnel that continued on the other side, he saw a trio of lights wavering in the blackness. Snatches of voice reached them from across the station, echoing in the huge space.

Without another word, the four of them crouched down. Their lights were still off, so they were in darkness here. A few of the shanties stood between them and the flashlights.

As the lights grew closer, the voices became clearer. George gulped. He recognized one of them. It was the man who had been threatening the boy. He still couldn't make out what anyone was saying, though.

The men came into the light at the other end of the station. Now George could see that they had the boy with them again. One of them was dragging the kid by his ear. The boy stumbled along, his neck twisted by the force of the thug's pull. Then the guy slapped his hand across the kid's face, the force throwing him into a chair. Another man began to tie him up again.

George crept closer, staying out of the light. He had to hear what they were saying. He felt exposed, even though he knew that the men couldn't see into the darkness. Not with those huge, bright construction lights glaring in their faces.

"I don't see why we have to bother with him anymore," one of the men grumbled. "Just let him go."

"Get rid of him, I say. He's caused too much trouble," another one added.

"You don't have a say, Sam," the boss guy said.

"Just be quiet and follow orders. He's got to prove he's telling the truth."

"The truth?" Sam snorted. "But we've got it. It was right where he said it was."

Got what? George wondered. He listened even harder.

The boss shook his head. "What if it's a fake?"

"Oh. I didn't think of that."

"No, you didn't think, Sam," he said. "That's why Leroy put me in charge instead of you. So just stay here with the kid while we check it out."

George crept closer as they finished tying up the boy. He looked even dirtier than he had the first time. And in the sharpness of the lights, George could see a defeated look on his face.

The guy in charge and the other man climbed from the tracks onto the station platform. The stairs there must have led up to street level long ago. The two disappeared up the steps.

George looked back at his three friends. This was their chance to rescue the boy—only one man was left guarding him. But how would they manage it? Even if he was only one guy, he still looked pretty tough.

Then George finally realized what he had to do.

He started to pick his way forward, staying in the shadows. Out of the corner of his eye, he could see Derrick and Shannon gesturing to him. George touched his finger to his lips. He moved to one side, slipping under the overhang of the platform. He remembered that his father had once told him about the crawl spaces beneath subway platforms. If you accidentally fell off the platform while a train was coming, you could jump into a nook alongside the tracks. They were just wide enough so the train wouldn't hit you as it passed.

Of course, the darkness below the platforms also hid old garbage thrown away by subway riders. Rats, too. Crawl space or not, George made it a point never to stand close to the edge.

He crept closer to the man and his captive. The bright lights were overhead, and he felt horribly exposed. But the man was facing the other way, his gaze focused on some spot across the station.

Then George realized where the man was looking. He was watching the hole the four of them had come through.

George gulped. He was watching for them. If they had started a half hour later, the man would have spotted Shannon the moment she stuck her head up. Good thing this was Operation: Midnight and not Operation: Twelve-thirty!

George stopped. He was right underneath the stairs the other two men had taken. He felt a trickle of sweat roll down his back. The ball of nerves in his stomach tightened. That was good. He was always better at this when he was nervous.

George raised his hands to his mouth.

"Sam! Get up here, *now*!" he yelled.

The guy spun around, looking up at the stairs. George's shoulders sagged with relief. He had nailed it! His voice had sounded exactly like the boss's voice. And with all the echoes in the vast station, it was impossible to tell where it had come from.

Sam scrambled onto the platform, jumping up only yards from where George crouched, and ran to the stairs. He took one look back at the captive boy. But the kid was tied up tight. Without another glance, Sam disappeared up the stairs.

George waited for a count of ten, then ran to the kid. Derrick and Shannon were already pounding down the tunnel.

"Genius idea." Shannon panted as she ran up. "But it was too risky. You could've been caught."

"Yeah, well, then you would have had to rescue *me*. An oath's an oath, right?"

Shannon smiled. "I guess so."

George pulled at the knots on the back side of

the chair in frustration. They wouldn't budge.

The kid stared up at him with steely eyes. His skin was so dirty, it was impossible to guess what it really looked like. On the other hand, his clothes weren't dirty so much as gray, as if the dirt that had been pounded into them was permanent. He smelled like freshly turned earth.

The kid didn't say a word.

Renee rushed up behind him. "Here, let me," she whispered, pushing George aside.

Her fingers made short work of the knots, and the rope fell into a pile around the kid's ankles. But he didn't move. He just sat there, glaring at them.

"Hey, man," Derrick said. "We just rescued you."

The boy was silent.

"Are you okay?" Renee asked, reaching out one hand to touch his shoulder.

The boy flinched. One arm swung out and batted away Renee's hand with a *smack.*

"Ouch!" she cried.

Suddenly, the kid was a blur of motion. He leaped from the chair and thrust one elbow into Derrick's stomach, crumpling him to the ground.

"Wait!" George shouted. "We just—"

The kid shot past him and ran toward the shantytown. George turned and dashed after him. *"Wait!"*

George pursued the kid the length of the station. The boy was taller than George, and he moved quickly. Taking long strides down the subway tracks, George could barely keep up. It wasn't until he reached the edge of the shantytown that he felt his ankle start to scream with agony.

"Owww!" he moaned, stumbling to a halt. He'd forgotten all about his injury.

He stared after the boy, who quickly disappeared into the blackness ahead. The kid never slowed his pace, as if he could see in the dark.

"You're welcome," George called after him. He sighed and turned back toward the station.

Renee and Shannon were bent over Derrick, who was rising gingerly to his knees. The kid must have knocked the wind right out of him. George flinched at the thought of one of those sharp, skinny elbows jabbing into his stomach.

He took a few limping steps back toward the station, then froze.

All three of the men were hurrying swiftly and silently down the stairs!

Twelve
Alone

George took a deep breath, about to shout a warning, but Shannon looked up and spotted the men. Without missing a beat, she pulled Derrick up and sprinted toward the hole.

"Look! The kid's gone!" the boss yelled.

Renee peered down the station toward George, but he could tell she couldn't see him in the darkness of the tunnel. She raised her hands to her mouth, about to call.

Don't! he thought. With his injured ankle, there was no way for him to escape by running. He had to hide.

He flicked on the light of his miner's helmet and frantically shook his head. The other three had to get down the hole *now*. Renee had to understand what he meant. *Don't try to help me. Don't let them know I'm here!*

He turned the helmet light off again, hoping the men hadn't spotted it.

The three men had reached the edge of the platform. One was jumping onto the tracks. Shannon and Derrick were already down the hole. Renee turned and ran after them, disappearing down into the tunnel below the station. She had understood.

George watched helplessly as the men followed them. They probably thought that the kid had gone down the hole with Shannon, Renee, and Derrick. George hoped his friends could stay ahead of them through the dark tunnels. This time, the men wouldn't be so easily put off by the threat of Kidd's traps.

George shuddered. Those guys had been scary enough when they'd just caught him spying on them. They'd be really angry now.

But Shannon, Renee, and Derrick still had a chance. They had covered the sloping tunnel three times now, and they had Kidd's map. They could squeeze through the tight passages more easily. Being bigger and stronger wasn't necessarily an advantage down here in the underworld.

George just hoped Derrick was okay. He'd looked bad, but with any luck the kid had just knocked the wind out of him.

When the last of the three men had disappeared down the hole, George found himself alone at the edge of the huge subway station. Where should he go now? He definitely wasn't sticking around here. The men might come back at any time.

He could go up the stairs of the subway station, where the men had gone. Maybe they led to the surface. But George doubted it. Since the station was abandoned, its entrance would almost certainly be boarded up. And he didn't want to go in any direction that the men might follow.

That left only one choice. He had to continue down the tunnel, the way the kid had gone.

He sighed and turned toward the darkness. Flicking on his helmet light, he trudged painfully forward.

The shanties surrounded him, as sad and empty as a ghost town. In the wavering light of his helmet, the jumble of walls looked like something out of a bad dream. George wondered again what had scared off the people who'd lived here. You'd have to be pretty tough to survive in this world of rats and darkness. So whatever had chased away the shantytown occupants must have been someone, or something, pretty frightening.

Whatever it was, George hoped he didn't run into it.

He thought about the boy again. They'd gone to all this trouble to rescue him, and the kid hadn't even said thank-you. Of course, he was probably out of practice. He must have been down here a long time. Maybe he'd even grown up down here.

Did he even know about the world aboveground? That would be really horrible—never seeing the sun, running around in these tunnels your whole life, trying to survive without anyone to protect you or maps to tell you where to go.

Maps! George thought. Of course. He still had Captain Kidd's map. He dug it out of his pocket and unfolded it.

With one finger, he traced the path they'd taken: downstream from George's house, up the sloping tunnel from the trap that Shannon had set off. Then to the eye symbol, the old trap that led to the subway station.

Wait. Subway station?

George smacked himself on the forehead. Of course, this map didn't make sense anymore. The subway hadn't been around in Kidd's day. The spot the map used to lead to might not even exist today. This map was three hundred years out-of-date. The underground world had gotten a lot more complicated when the subways and sewer systems and all the other stuff down here had been built.

He folded the map back up and put it in his pocket. It had seemed like such a great discovery when they'd found it in his attic. But now it seemed about as useful as an invitation to a party that had happened last year.

George kept walking. At least he had the sub-way tracks to follow. They must lead *somewhere*.

He looked up at the walls, and his helmet light showed another of the warning signs:

FOLLOW LEROY'S RULES OR PAY THE PRICE!

Great, George thought. Leroy's rules. No one had bothered to tell him the rules. Or the price, for that matter. All he had to go on was a three-hundred-year-old map and some crazy writing on the wall.

For a moment, George almost wished he'd grown up in a house *without* a history. *Without* a secret door.

Suddenly, he heard a rumbling sound and swal-lowed. It was a noise he had known all his life. A subway train was coming.

He peered frantically down the tunnel, looking for a train's headlights. But he couldn't see anything.

Of course not, he realized. The train wasn't on this track. It had been abandoned a long time ago. The homeless people had built shelters on it and everything. But the noise got louder and louder, the tracks under his feet rumbling like in an earthquake.

The train must be somewhere close by but not here, George's mind insisted. But he couldn't shake the idea that he was standing right in the path of an approaching train. An awful fear grew along with the sound. His palms felt clammy.

Maybe it was some kind of ghost train, still haunting the old tunnel, still carrying ghostly passengers between stops. He looked both ways, half expecting to see a phantom train bearing down on him.

Nothing but darkness.

Finally, the rumbling sound passed, fading away into nothing again.

George laughed aloud with relief. No ghost train, just another tunnel close by. He should be thankful that he could hear something. Maybe he was close to a real station, with stairs that led back to the surface. That train had probably been full of people coming home from late parties or going to work at night jobs. He reminded himself that a whole city was very close. A familiar street was probably just a few yards away through the concrete over his head. The rumble of the subway was proof of that.

Wait! he thought. *Just a few yards of concrete . . .* He'd forgotten about his walkie-talkie. Renee had said the signal could go through rocks and concrete. George pulled it from the belt and switched it on.

"Come in, Renee."

The speaker made a few little pops but said nothing.

"Shannon? Derrick?"

Still nothing. He wondered what that meant. Had his friends been captured? Maybe they were just too far away. Or they might still be trying to escape. If they were running, they wouldn't have had time to turn on their walkie-talkies.

George left the device on and kept walking.

After a couple hundred feet, he left the shanties behind. The tracks disappeared, too. All that was left were the wooden ties, ripped up and left in a jumble. George had to pick his way carefully across them. Probably the metal rails had been torn out and used somewhere else or melted down for scrap. The tunnel felt much spookier without them. It was as if the world had been completely destroyed and George was the last person left.

George checked his watch. "Whoa," he muttered. It was after one o'clock in the morning. At least time was still passing by. Down here, it felt like the night had been frozen in place.

For the first time all night, he felt tired. The excitement of the adventure was wearing off, leaving simple fear and exhaustion.

If they had escaped, Shannon, Renee, and Derrick should have gotten back to the secret door by now. They would be in his basement. He tried the walkie-talkie again. Nothing.

He swallowed his fear. Maybe he was just out of range. Yeah, that must be it.

They were probably trying to figure out what to do, planning another rescue mission. But it wouldn't be easy since they didn't know where he was.

For that matter, *George* didn't know where he was.

He looked at the compass on his watch. He was walking northeast now, headed right up the island of Manhattan. Sooner or later this tunnel had to lead *somewhere*.

Suddenly, George heard a sound behind him, a far-off click of stone against stone.

He spun around, his helmet light sweeping across the walls. Down the dark tunnel, he thought he saw a tiny spark of light, but it disappeared before his eyes could be sure. He stared hard but couldn't see anything.

So he was seeing things now. George wondered for a moment if he had imagined the sound of the passing train, too. Maybe being alone in all this darkness was driving him crazy. His mind must be making up sights and sounds to fill the black, empty spaces around him.

But he was pretty sure he had seen something.

George turned back the way he'd been going. He started walking again, trying to focus on the exit that must be somewhere ahead. But as he made his way across the jumble of uprooted ties, he couldn't shake the feeling that someone was behind him.

He tried to move more quickly, but his ankle screamed whenever he went faster than a walk. Whoever was behind him, he couldn't outrun them.

What if it were one of his friends? No—they would be calling his name, wouldn't they? And they'd turn their walkie-talkies on, too. And why had the light disappeared the moment he turned around?

He thought of spinning around again, too quickly for his pursuer to turn off the light. If George caught a glimpse of the light again, at least he'd know he wasn't going crazy. But whoever it was would also know that George had become suspicious.

George decided he didn't want his pursuer to know that *he* knew he was being followed. He kept walking and figured out a plan.

Without slowing down, George reached up to unstrap the miner's helmet. He carefully held it with both hands, crouching down to duck out of it. He kept walking, holding it above him at head height, the helmet still facing the way he'd been going.

But he turned his head to glance over his shoulder.

He shivered when he saw it. He hadn't been crazy. The light was there behind him, flickering among the track ties.

Someone was following him.

And that someone had gotten closer.

George stumbled, banging his sore ankle against a track tie. He had to bite his tongue to keep from letting out a yell of pain. He'd better watch where he was going. But his spine crawled now with the thought of the shadowy pursuer.

What was he going to do?

Sooner or later, the person behind him was going to catch up. With his bad ankle, George couldn't walk any faster, much less run. With his helmet light on, there was no way to miss him. If he turned it off, plunging himself into darkness, he would be blind and unable to move.

Either way, the person following him would reach him eventually.

He kept walking, holding the helmet above his head, racking his brain for an idea.

Suddenly, George felt a warm breeze against his face.

He turned to face the draft without turning the light toward it. In a bit of reflected light, he could just see a crack in the tunnel wall. The hole was a ragged black triangle in the gray concrete, as tall as George and maybe a foot wide. A stain of dripping water descended from it.

George kept moving, thinking furiously. Could he

crawl into that hole? Would he really fit? He didn't know what might be in there or how far back it went. And from his brief glimpse, George wasn't even sure it was deep enough for him to squeeze into and hide.

But it didn't seem like he had any other choice.

George thought of movies in which an escaping prisoner would double back, fooling a pack of bloodhounds that were tracking his scent. If he could just make it back to the gap, whoever was behind him would walk straight past him—if he was lucky.

He walked on another ten seconds, strapping his helmet back onto his head. He would need his hands free.

He took a deep breath, then suddenly turned around again.

Again, the light behind him flicked off instantly.

George reached up and turned off his own light.

The tunnel was now totally dark. In the blackness, images flickered across George's vision, as if he were rubbing his eyes. He could somehow feel his pursuer staring back at him through the void.

Whoever it was would be wondering what George was up to.

He crouched down and started moving, picking his way carefully back toward the gap in the tunnel wall. He waved his hands in front of him, feeling for the track ties. Now every step forward was treacherous.

George's knee banged against something hard once, but he managed to stifle the cry that came to his lips. He had to make it to the gap without being heard or seen.

No sound or light came from the pursuer. The tunnel stayed dark. Maybe whoever it was thought that George would eventually have to turn on his light again.

Or maybe the other person was getting closer every second, moving with absolute silence through the darkness. George imagined a hand suddenly reaching out of the blackness and grabbing him. He swallowed nervously and kept moving, chills running up and down his spine.

After agonizing moments, George felt the warm breeze coming from the hole. He turned toward it and took a few blind steps. His hands found the wall and then the edges of the gap. He put one foot carefully forward.

His sneaker squished softly into cold water, and George shivered. He pulled himself in, one hand against the rocky side, the other feeling for something in front of his face.

The gap narrowed, but it was big enough for him to pull himself in a bit farther. A glimmer of light reached his eyes. The wet walls of the crack glistened, and behind him the black tunnel held a dancing beam of light. His pursuer had grown tired of waiting and was looking for him again.

George had made it to the gap just in time.

George's eyes had adjusted over the last minutes to the blackness. In the reflected glow, he could even see a few inches in front of him. The gap was bigger than he'd thought and seemed to go back pretty far. The breeze had to be coming from somewhere. He squeezed forward, and the water dripping down the walls soaked through his T-shirt like cold fingers prodding him.

Then, suddenly, he was stuck. His rope-climbing harness was wedged tight between two walls of rock. He tried to move forward, then backward, but the walls were closed in on him like a giant fist. It felt like they were moving, slowly crushing him.

Maybe he had stumbled into one of Kidd's traps!

George got control of himself quickly. Even Captain Kidd couldn't have made walls that moved, he told himself. The walls *weren't* moving. He was just stuck. He breathed out, emptying his lungs of air. By making himself as skinny as possible, he was able to inch forward until he suddenly popped free.

Wherever he was now, the warm breeze was stronger. Somehow, the space *felt* big around him.

The sound of dripping water echoed softly around him. *I must be in some kind of cave,* he thought.

Light flickered from back in the tunnel. It was much closer now. He could tell by the strength of the beam.

George knelt and peered around the edge of the cave mouth. The crunch of footsteps on the gravel floor of the tunnel reached his ears. Whoever it was moved slowly. The flashlight was sweeping back and forth, probing every corner, searching. Searching for him.

George's stomach fluttered as the footsteps grew closer.

Then the beam of light found the gap in the tunnel wall. George pulled back into the shadows. His breath caught in his chest.

The footsteps grew closer, and light swelled in the gap. George could see the golden light fall on his own hands. He felt frozen, like a rabbit facing a huge snake.

A slithering sound reached his ears. Someone was squeezing into the gap, clothes rasping against the slimy walls. George could hear the man's breathing, deep and heavy. Then a grunt, followed by a low, frustrated muttering.

The man was stuck!

George let his breath out softly with relief. His

pursuer was too big to get through the tight spot. He was safe here.

The muttering went on as the man struggled, and George realized that he couldn't understand the words. Maybe the underworld had its own language, a secret tongue that had been slowly created over the years.

The man struggled for another minute, and a terrible thought entered George's head. What if the man was completely stuck? What if he never freed himself? George would be stuck here with him, trapped, as if he'd been stuffed into a giant bottle that had then been corked.

But after another moment's struggle, the man pulled himself free, stumbling back into the tunnel. George heard him muttering angrily in his unknown language.

Then he heard the man slowly move away.

George was safe.

He sighed quietly. All he had to do was wait until the man had gone farther down the tunnel, and he could slip out of the gap and go the other way. Maybe he could even make it back to the subway station. If no one was there, he'd be able to follow the map back to his house. But he had to wait here for a while, until the man went a long way down the subway tunnel.

George was desperate for light, but he didn't dare turn on his headlamp yet, and he knew better than to explore the cave in the dark. The echoes made it sound big, and he didn't want to lose track of where the narrow opening was. He wished he had the range-finding device, but Renee had kept it with her.

So he sat down in the dark and listened to the sounds of the cave around him. The *drip, drip* of water came from somewhere nearby. The breeze blowing past him made a soft shushing noise. And at the edge of his hearing, he heard something disturb the rocks.

George swallowed. Were there rats in here? He rose to his feet.

Suddenly, something moved behind him. Something *big*.

He started to cry out, but then a cold hand clamped over his mouth.

Thirteen
PAUL

George fought to tear the hand away from his mouth, but another closed over his face. He could hardly breathe!

George wrenched open his mouth and chomped down on the hand. It tasted like dirt and felt as calloused and hard as leather. Nothing George did seemed to have an effect. Even clawing and biting with all his strength, he couldn't break free.

There was only one thing he could try. George shut his eyes, reached up, and flicked on his helmet light. Even through closed eyes he could see the blinding light that flooded the tiny chamber.

His attacker let out a strangled scream, and George felt the hands drop away from his face. He peeked at his attacker through slitted eyes. It was the kid they'd rescued!

He fell onto the ground, curling up and covering his eyes. "Ow!" he moaned. "Make it dark. Make it dark!"

George knelt and straddled the boy, forcing him down against the rocky floor. He turned off his helmet light. It was like a thousand camera flashes had all gone off at once. All George could see was a bright blue spot right in front of his eyes.

"Stupid," the boy hissed. "Leroy will see."

George heard footsteps returning outside. Had the man seen the light? Or heard the sounds of their struggle?

The two of them froze. George tried to blink away the blue spots that swarmed in his vision. Had the man heard them? If he knew someone was in here, he could just wait outside. George would be trapped.

Or would he? The boy had come from somewhere.

There was a grunt from the gap. The man was trying to squeeze through again.

The boy was whispering something very softly. George knelt closer.

"Follow me."

He gulped. But in this situation there was no choice. He had to trust the kid, even though he had just tried to smother him.

George let him up slowly, expecting the boy to strike out at any moment. But the kid grasped his hand and pulled him away from the gap. George followed, feeling the breeze on his face. They were moving toward the back of the cave.

A stone slipped under George's foot.

"Quiet!" the boy whispered.

Easy for you to say, George thought. The kid had silently sneaked up on him when George had been listening as hard as he could. Anyone who could get around so quickly and quietly must have grown up in a strange, dangerous world.

The boy pulled George forward quickly, as if they were walking down a brightly lit hallway instead of through a crooked, pitch-black cave. George's feet splashed into cold, wet patches, and the dripping sound was everywhere. His helmet bumped against rocky outcroppings once or twice, drawing more soft complaints from the kid.

When he was sure they were at least a hundred feet away from the subway tunnel, George whispered, "Let me turn on my light."

"*No.* Leroy's man will see it. He's not day-blind like you."

"Day-blind?" George's sore ankle buckled, and he caught himself with a wince.

"From being out in the dayside. And using brights. It makes your eyes weak." The kid had a weird way of talking, as if he came from a foreign country. There were kids from around the world at George's school, but the boy's accent wasn't any that George recognized.

"But I can't see *anything* down here."

"You will, if you wait. Every time you see a bright, it takes your eyes a thousand counts to go back to normal."

Normal? George thought. He thought about when he'd been on a field trip up to the Columbia University observatory one night to look at the stars. Before they used the telescope, the teacher had turned off all the lights in the classroom, using only a dim, red-tinted flashlight to lead the way. It had taken about twenty minutes before everyone's eyes had completely adjusted to the darkness.

Of course, for this kid, night vision must be "normal." Down here in the darkness, that would make sense. And twenty minutes was about a thousand seconds, or "counts."

Maybe Derrick was right. Being down here *was* a lot like being in a different world. A secret underground world where nothing worked the same.

"Who's Leroy?" George whispered.

"He makes the rules down here. Didn't you see the signs?"

"You mean all that graffiti? Yeah," George said. "But who *is* he?"

"He's Leroy," the boy said. "He showed up a long time ago. Back when I was little. And he just took over. He and his men started pushing everyone around. Most of my people left."

"Why is he here?"

"He has his reasons. His people hid things down here. You know, things from the dayside."

George didn't know what to make of the boy's answers, but he still had more questions.

"Why were you tied up? What did he want from you?"

"The less you know about that, the safer you will find yourself. The danger is already too much."

"What do you mean?" George asked. The kid's grasp tightened on George's hand, but he remained silent.

George bumped his head again, the helmet thunking against rock.

"That's what you get for using brights all the time," the boy said. "I can see just fine now."

"Good for you," George muttered.

As they walked, George gradually started to see glimmers, too. Light was coming from some-where. The wet walls of the tunnel glinted coldly. George checked his watch again. Not even 2 A.M. yet. He felt like he'd been down here in the dark for hours.

"What's your name, anyway?" he asked.

The kid didn't say anything.

"Mine's George," he offered.

"Paul," the boy said after a pause.

Paul? That sounded normal enough. Somehow, knowing his name made George feel more com-fortable. He reminded himself that Paul was just a kid like him. Only he'd grown up in an incredibly weird place.

George's mind filled with questions. How had Paul wound up down here? How had he learned to read? What did he eat?

"Paul?" he asked. "Do you have parents?"

There was a long, silent moment.

"I had a mother," Paul finally said. "She died a long time ago. We came down here when I was really little. To escape this man."

"You mean Leroy?"

"No. My father."

George didn't know how to reply. "My mom died, too," he blurted.

"That's too bad," Paul said. "But if you don't shut up, you could die tonight. Leroy will hear you."

George heeded the warning. As he carefully followed Paul, his mind filled with images of his mother. For once, he didn't want to think about her, not down here in this dark place. The blackness suddenly seemed to be crushing him. He kept his eyes focused on Paul, trying to anticipate his next steps.

George was surprised when Paul broke the silence. "My mom died right after Leroy got here," he said. "There was an old woman who took me in then. She wasn't the nicest person, but she taught me how to live down here. She knew the tunnels better than Mom. And she knew how to follow the rules and stay away from dayside people."

So some people were kind down here. Someone had taken care of Paul. George guessed they all had to stick together in this unlit world, and they obviously didn't like people from above. George had no idea where Paul was taking him, but he felt he had to trust him.

"So, why did you grab me back there?"

"I was coming to get you. To help you get back to the dayside. You don't belong here. You are not safe. Leroy's new man was following you. The one who only came a few months ago. The one who brought Leroy all the weapons and special tools."

Weapons and special tools? *For what?* George wondered. *Treasure hunting?*

"That new man is not like the others," Paul continued. "He's more dangerous. You needed my help."

"Help? You practically suffocated me!" George protested.

"You were going to scream. He would have heard you and come back," Paul said.

"Well, he didn't."

Paul whirled around to face George. "What are you doing down here, anyway? You don't belong."

"You know," George said, his voice rising, "we came down here to *rescue* you."

Paul didn't say anything.

"Which you didn't exactly bother to thank us for," George added.

"So what made you think I needed rescuing?"

George hesitated. He wasn't sure how much to tell Paul about the treasure hunt.

"Well, we saw you two days ago. Those guys— Leroy's men—were questioning you. It sounded like they were forcing you to tell them where something was. It seemed like you needed our help because it didn't sound like you were going to tell them."

He heard the boy sigh in defeat.

"You told them?" George asked.

"I did. And now Leroy has it. You rescued me too late."

George gritted his teeth. "Well, at least you're not tied to that chair anymore. What were you trying to hide, anyway?"

"Something I found."

Paul turned back around and kept going.

By now, George could see well enough to walk without Paul's hand guiding him. Light was coming from in front of them. They'd been climbing for the last few minutes. It seemed like they were getting closer to the surface. A new sound reached George's ears, a soft swooshing. Maybe it was traffic?

"Are you taking me up to the . . . dayside?"

"Yes. I told you, you don't belong. Why did you come down here in the first place?"

George thought for a second. Something told him he should be honest with Paul. "We were looking for buried treasure. See, we found this map . . ." he began.

The boy stopped moving so suddenly that George bumped into him.

"A map? Where did you get it?" Paul demanded.

George was startled. "It was in my house," he explained. "I mean, it had been in my family for a long time. But no one knew about it until me and my friends found it."

Paul nodded slowly, then turned away again and gestured for George to follow.

Around a corner, George could see where the light had been coming from. He looked up. He could see the bars of a sewer grate and the cold glow of a streetlight spilling through.

Paul flinched as if it were a spotlight aimed at his face. "Don't look straight at it! It's bad for your eyes."

George laughed, still looking up. The fresh, warm air of a spring night drifted down. He had never smelled anything so wonderful.

"I'm just happy to see light. I wasn't sure if I ever would again."

George looked for a ladder or some way to get up to the grate. "How do I get up there?"

"The exit is close by."

George looked at Paul expectantly. He didn't move.

"What do you want?" George asked.

"Can I see your map?"

George felt a sudden jolt of fear. Why did Paul want to see the map? What if he took it from him and just left him down here underground? George was close to the surface, but he still didn't know how to get out.

"And then you'll show me how to get back to the dayside?" he said cautiously. "I've got to find out if my friends are okay."

"Of course. I told you that you don't belong here. It isn't safe for me or you."

George wondered if Paul would use the map to find the treasure without them. Paul knew his way around down here much better than they did. Of course, the map was three hundred years out-of-date. He and the others had already reached a dead end. Maybe Paul could help them.

"One condition," he said.

Paul's eyes narrowed. "What?"

"The map shows the way to a secret treasure. If I show it to you, you have to help us find it. Not just take it for yourself."

"I don't have to help you," Paul said.

"I don't have to show you the map." George hoped he sounded tougher than he felt.

Paul looked closely at him. "Okay. I'll help you if I can."

"Swear?"

"I swear."

George spat into his hand and held it out. Paul looked at him like he was crazy.

"Oh, never mind," George said, wiping his hand on his pants. He pulled out the map and handed it to Paul.

The boy studied it for a moment.

"It's different," he murmured. "But kind of the same. I recognize this." He pointed to a symbol on the map: the skull and crossbones, or the Jolly Roger. George leaned down to look.

"You recognize that symbol? From where?"

Paul shrugged. "A place in the tunnels. There's a room with a lot of junk." He looked at George. "This was in your house?"

George nodded. "Um, Paul, you just said this map was 'different.' Different than what?"

Paul shook his head. "I don't know what it means. I don't know where it starts."

"Let me show you," George said. He bent over the map, his head close to Paul's. "This line is a stream that goes west."

"West?" Paul gave him a blank stare.

"Um. Let's try again. You know that old subway station you were tied up in? This tunnel runs into it. My friends and I came out of a hole not too far from where you were tied up."

"Yes, you stuck your head out of it when I was tied up." A faint smile crossed Paul's face. "You yelled when you saw the crawler."

The crawler? "Oh, right. The rat," George said. "I don't see a lot of rats close up like that. Anyway, that hole would be right about here. I think this tunnel is supposed to go farther, see? It goes up, and there's a tunnel that branches off and goes off the side of the map. If you stay in the first tunnel, it leads right to the X. But when they built the subway . . ."

Paul nodded, taking the map back from him. He stared at it intensely.

"I know where the rest of that tunnel is."

"Really?" George asked, his heartbeat picking up.

"Yes. There's a hole in the top of the subway station. It must have been the same tunnel a long time ago. I can take you there now."

"Now? But I've got to find out where my friends are."

"Now. Now is the only time I can help you."

George bit his lip. Paul made sense. What were they going to do, make a date for later? Paul didn't have a clock or a phone. He measured time in "counts," and without the sun they couldn't even have days down here. If he wanted Paul's help, he'd have to take it now.

But George didn't know if the other three had made it away from Leroy's men. And his friends were more important than any treasure. He had to get home.

He bit his lip. "Never mind, then."

"Okay," Paul said. He gestured for George to follow.

Around a corner, they emerged into a man-made tunnel. At the other end, George could see the silhouettes of trees. Where were they? Had they left the city altogether?

Paul squinted in the moonlight streaming down the tunnel.

"Thank you for rescuing me, George," he said.

"No problem. Thanks for getting me back to the dayside—even though it's nighttime. So, good-bye, I guess."

Paul looked solemnly at him.

"You shouldn't come back down, George. You don't belong."

George nodded. All he wanted now was to go home. "Maybe you're right."

"Yes. Good-bye."

"Good-bye, Paul."

"George?" came a tiny voice.

Paul jumped back, looking down at George's tool belt.

"Shannon to George," the voice came again.

His walkie-talkie had crackled to life.

Fourteen

George pulled the walkie-talkie from his belt and fumbled to press the talk button. "Shannon!" he answered.

"George, is that you?"

"Yeah! Are you guys okay? Where are you?"

"I'm in a cab."

"You're *what*?"

"Well, we've been trying to get you by walkie-talkie, but you were out of range," she explained. "Then Renee had an idea. She figured if we moved around the city, we might get to a place close enough to you to pick up your signal."

"Smart."

"We're all in different cabs, driving around. Where are *you*?"

"Uh, I'm not sure." George looked out the mouth of the tunnel. He could see a river glistening ahead of him, with buildings on the other side. "I'm looking at a river. Maybe the East River."

"Nope," Shannon said. Her voice was getting

clearer all the time. "I'm on the West Side. You must be looking at the Hudson."

"I'm in a park. Grass and trees and stuff."

Shannon thought for a second and then said, "Hudson River Park!"

"Must be."

"I'll tell the others. We'll meet you in twenty minutes."

George lowered his walkie-talkie and turned to Paul, excitement building inside him.

"My friends are okay! They'll be here in . . . about a thousand counts. Do you still want to find that treasure?"

Paul shrugged. "I don't care about the treasure."

George sighed. "How can you not care about the treasure, Paul? If you found the treasure, you could . . . you could . . ." *You could get out of here,* George thought, looking into the gloomy tunnels. But he didn't say anything. Paul was so used to life in the tunnels, he was probably afraid of anything else.

"Your friends are coming back to find the treasure?" Paul asked.

"Uh-huh."

Paul nodded. "I'll help you," he seemed to decide right then. "At least if you get the treasure, I know you won't come back down."

*   *   *

Twenty minutes later, they were all together at the end of the tunnel.

"That was a fifteen-dollar cab ride!" Derrick complained. "And all I did was go in circles."

"Okay, if Captain Kidd's treasure is only fifteen bucks, you get it all," Shannon said.

"No, we took an oath. We split everything we find evenly," George said. He turned to Paul. "That means you get a share, too, if you join us."

The boy shrugged. "I don't want treasure. I just want Leroy to go away."

"You mean the leader of those thugs? I'm all for ruining his day," Shannon said.

"How did you get away from them?" George asked.

She snorted. "Those guys are way slow," she said. "Without you along to hold us up, they never stood a chance."

"Thanks a lot," George said. "Well, let's get started."

Paul led them back into the tunnel. When they were inside, Renee turned on her flashlight.

"Turn it off!" Paul cried.

Renee looked at George, who covered his eyes.

"Just keep the lights off," he said. "Paul's right. You don't need lights if you just let your eyes adjust."

"Are you kidding?" Shannon asked.

"Trust me."

They moved forward in darkness. They were still in the sewer tunnels, just below the surface, so patches of moonlight poured in through the sewer grates over their heads. Paul covered his eyes around these "brights," and Derrick, Shannon, and Renee looked at George in puzzlement. He shrugged.

George knew his friends were troubled by Paul's presence. Derrick was still angry about being punched in the gut after the rescue. And Paul *was* pretty weird. His dirty skin and strange way of talking took some getting used to.

But they had all accepted George's word that he was a friend. The four of them had been through enough to trust one another now.

George tried to keep track of where they were going. They headed east, toward the middle of town, then south, back in the direction of his house. He was glad when he realized that these tunnels weren't for sewage, but just to drain water from the streets when it rained. In a few places, though, they did smell pretty bad. Paul never hesitated at a fork in the tunnels, as if he were going for a walk in a familiar neighborhood. *Of course, this* was *Paul's neighborhood,* George realized.

His ankle felt much better. Renee had wrapped the bandage tightly again, and resting while he'd waited for the other three to arrive had helped. He could walk without limping now.

He was getting pretty sleepy, though. His watch said it was almost 4 A.M. It was going to be fun trying to stay awake in school.

After a half hour of walking, they reached a place where the storm drain started to slope downward. Cracks appeared in the concrete around them, as if the tunnel had collapsed long ago.

Paul took them farther down. It grew darker, but their eyes slowly adjusted. George pressed the button on his watch and found that even its tiny light was like a glaring beacon down here. He scanned the walls with it. This part of the tunnel was crumbling, the concrete broken through in places.

Finally, Paul pointed to a gap in the concrete that was big enough to crawl into. Water dripped from it, and it was green with what looked like algae.

"Great," Derrick said. "Is this the only way down?"

"Yes," Paul said. "This leads down to a hole in the roof of the abandoned subway station. It must be the rest of the tunnel that's on your map."

"The one with the X on it," Derrick said.

"Yeah, that one," George said. "Okay. I'll go first."

"You're always going first," Shannon argued. "You got to have a whole adventure with Paul while we were riding around in stupid taxis. I'm going first."

Without another word, Shannon crawled into the gap.

"Ewww, this water's cold," she complained.

Derrick called down to her, "Don't forget what it showed on the map. There was an eye symbol. You might find another trap down there. Be careful."

"Yeah, I remember. George, it's so dark down here," Shannon said. "I can't really be careful if I can't see anything."

"Paul," George said. "We need to use our brights now. We can't see as well as you."

Paul nodded. "This is as far as I'm going, anyway. I hope you find your treasure, but you shouldn't come down here again." He turned to Derrick. "Sorry I hit you. Thanks for rescuing me."

Then he turned away and walked down the tunnel.

"Bye," George said as Paul disappeared into the gloom.

"He was pretty cool," Derrick said. "For someone who lives underground."

"Okay, Shannon," George called. "You can use your light now."

A few seconds later, light poured from the hole. They all covered their eyes for a moment.

"Ow," Derrick said, squinting. "Maybe that kid's got the right idea."

"Yeah, I think we're all a little day-blind," George agreed.

"A little what?"

"Never mind." He switched on his own helmet light and pointed it at the hole. "Let's go."

One by one, they followed Shannon. It was a natural tunnel, the walls made of rough granite. They had to crawl because the roof was only a few feet high. When the slope became steeper, they all turned around to go feetfirst. Going headfirst downhill was too scary, and they couldn't keep balanced.

"This is pretty tough. Maybe we should use some rope," George said to Renee.

"Sure. We'll just connect ourselves." She ran a length of rope among them, attached to all their harnesses.

"Great," said Shannon. "This way if anyone falls down a hole, everyone does."

They kept going. The cold water trickling down the tunnel's floor began to soak into the backside of George's pants. But he hardly noticed. He could feel somehow that they were close to the treasure.

It wasn't too long before Shannon called up in a harsh whisper, "Lights off."

The other three darkened their lights instantly. They all obeyed each other without question now, George noticed.

He scooted down next to Shannon. The two of them could just fit side by side in the tunnel.

"What is it?" he asked.

"Look."

Light was coming from just below them, shining up through the end of the tunnel. They crawled carefully forward and peeked over the edge.

It was the abandoned subway station, and they were above it. George could see the bank of construction lights and all the electronic equipment sitting on the tracks. He could see the hole that they had come through earlier that night to rescue Paul. It was lined up exactly with this tunnel. Paul had been right. This was the continuation of the tunnel on Kidd's map. It had been cut in two when the subway line was built.

He just hoped the treasure was still here, too.

From below, George could hear voices talking, but from this angle he couldn't see anyone. He strained to make out the words.

"I can't believe you let him get away."

"It doesn't matter. We've got it now."

"What about those other kids?"

"Don't worry. I'll deal with them."

Shannon and George looked at each other.

"Let's get the treasure and get out of here," George whispered.

"Well," Shannon whispered, "if it's here, it has to be behind us."

"You think we missed it?"

"This is as far as the tunnel goes, George."

"You're right. If it's not behind us, then . . ." He looked down. If Kidd's treasure wasn't in the tunnel behind them and it wasn't in the other part of the tunnel that they had already explored, then it must have been where the subway tunnel was now. Which meant it was gone forever.

He drew in a deep breath. "Okay, everyone. Let's look again."

The four of them crawled around in the tight space, searching every crevice carefully. The minutes slowly passed.

"It has to be here somewhere," Derrick hissed.

While he was searching, George dislodged a small, perfectly round pebble. He clenched his teeth as it rolled down the slope toward the hole. It came to a stop just before it went over the edge.

"Phew." The last thing they needed was to draw the attention of Leroy's men up here.

"Look!" Renee whispered suddenly.

All four of them scrambled over to where she was. In the light from the subway station, George could see the glint of metal embedded in the rock. This *had* to be it.

"Captain Kidd's treasure," he whispered.

His heart began to pound. Finally, they had found the X!

Renee brushed away loose dirt to reveal a small, rectangular metal plate.

"What is it, gold?" Derrick asked.

"No, it's just rusty steel," Renee said.

George remembered the metal grate that had dumped rocks on them the first time they'd been underground. "Careful! It might be one of Kidd's traps."

"I don't think so," Renee said. "It looks like there's a keyhole."

George squinted. She was right. In the center of the metal plate was a tiny slot, about the size of the key to his mailbox at home.

"Well, that's convenient," Derrick said. "Except we don't have the key."

They all stared at the little keyhole helplessly. George felt a surge of frustration. They were so close—but they couldn't get to the treasure!

"Hit it with something," Derrick said.

Renee tapped it with her hammer. It sounded solid. She hit it a bit harder.

"Shhh," George said. "Those guys are right below us. We don't want to make them suspicious. We need the key."

"A key!" Shannon complained. "We come all this way underground, face booby traps and bad guys, and we still need a *key*? Man, George, your great-whatever grandfather was a major pain."

"He wasn't my *grandfather*," George interrupted her. "I've explained this again and again. He married Sarah Oort, who was my mother's—" Suddenly, he broke off.

"All right, all right," Shannon said. "She was your great-times-eight grandmother. I get it."

"That's *it*!" George cried.

His friends looked at him in confusion. George reached into his pocket and fished around. A few moments later he pulled it out: the golden locket with his mother's portrait inside.

"The picture of my mother," George said. "I mean, Sarah Oort. That's the key."

Renee frowned. "Huh?"

"Remember what the map said?" George gently opened the heart-shaped locket and ran his finger over the carved surface of ivory. "'The key to good fortune lies in the heart.'"

Shannon's mouth dropped wide open. Renee peered at the keyhole, and Derrick looked at George eagerly.

"Open it!" Derrick said.

"I always thought that this was my mother," George murmured under his breath. "But I guess it was really made to look like Sarah Oort."

"Kidd's wife," Shannon said. "He loved her. That's what the clue means."

"Let me see," Renee said, reaching out for the locket.

"No!" George said, clenching it in his fist.

"George," she said softly. "My fingers are smaller than yours."

He looked at her for a second. It made sense— maybe the key was inside. But the locket was the only thing he owned of his mother's. It was hard to give up.

But he trusted Renee. It wasn't like she was going to steal the locket. Or laugh at him for always carrying it.

"Here." He gently placed the pendant in her hand. She fiddled with it for a few seconds.

Suddenly, the little portrait swung clear of its backing. Something silvery dropped into Renee's hand.

A tiny silver key.

George could hardly believe it. His whole life, he'd carried something that had been passed down from William Kidd himself. It had been right there, and he'd never known!

"The key to good fortune," Renee said, holding it up to the light.

"The key to *huge* fortune," Shannon added, laughing breathlessly. "Guys, can you believe this? We're about to become crazy rich!"

"Let's try it," Derrick said.

Renee handed the key to George. His fingers shook as he put it into the lock and turned it.

Nothing happened.

"Well," Derrick said. "That was a—"

Suddenly, the tunnel was filled with sound. George heard metal gears turning, grinding against three centuries of rust, old springs pushing outward against hard stone. The floor of the tunnel shook, and loose rocks streamed past them and into the subway station below.

Oh, man. The guys down there were definitely going to notice them now.

Then the tunnel started to tip, getting steeper and steeper. George felt himself sliding downward.

"It was a trap!" Derrick yelled.

"Grab onto something!" Shannon shouted.

George braced himself against the top and bottom of the tunnel, pushing hard in both directions so that he wouldn't slide down the slope. He was the one closest to the drop into the subway station.

But something was wrong. The tunnel's ceiling was higher than it had been a moment ago.

"The walls are moving!" cried George. The tunnel was getting wider. It was being pushed apart. He was losing his grip.

So Captain Kidd *could* make walls move after all!

"Look!" Renee said.

Around the metal plate, a crack was forming. George struggled to keep from sliding down the tunnel, his eyes riveted on the keyhole. The rock was splitting apart around it, opening up to reveal . . .

A book.

A *book*?

The rumbling slowly trailed off. The rock had opened up just enough to show an old, musty set of pages bound together with a rotting leather spine.

"It's just an old book!" Renee said.

"*That's* the treasure?" Derrick asked.

"Shhh!" George hissed. "Those guys are right down—"

Then, as he turned to point, his foot slipped out from under him.

With the loose rocks and dirt all around him, the sloping tunnel was like a water slide. He shot toward the hole, unable to grab anything, and rushed into open space.

"Ahhhhhh!" His scream was cut short by the jerk of the rope on his harness. George spun wildly in the air, the lights in the subway station whirling around him.

"What the—?"

"It's that kid again!"

George could see the men below him, looking up with shocked expressions. They must have noticed the rocks and dust spewing from the hole and thought it was an earthquake or something, but George was sure they hadn't expected to see him.

"Well, grab him, you idiots!"

He was dangling halfway to the station floor, just out of reach. The men raced toward him.

"Guys! Pull me up! Pull me up!" he yelled frantically.

"Hang on!" He heard Derrick's voice from above.

"I am hanging on!" George yelled.

The tallest man reached out one long arm. He grabbed George's foot. George kicked him with the other.

"Ow! You little—"

The man stepped back to take a running jump. He came down the tracks at George. But just as he leaped, George felt himself yanked upward. The man's grasping hands fell short.

"Yeah!" George shouted. "Keep pulling!"

He reached up to grab the rope in his hands. He started to climb, hand over hand. He pulled himself higher and higher. A crazy thought came to him: *He'd never gone this fast in gym class!*

Shannon, Renee, and Derrick were pulling the rope at the same time. In a few seconds, he was at the hole. Shannon reached through, grabbed his harness, and yanked him in.

Strangely, he decided his fear of falling was cured. "Whoa! What a ride!" he yelled.

Shannon looked at him like he was insane. The shouts of Leroy's men still came up through the hole. She dared a peek down.

"Uh-oh. We'd better go—now!"

"Wait!" George said. "Did someone get the book?"

Shannon tapped her jacket pocket. "Right here."

"Okay, let's go."

They scrambled back up the slope and into the drainage tunnel. It was easy to find their way back across town. At last, they emerged into Hudson River Park, leaving the underworld behind.

When they came out of the last tunnel, they all stopped short. The sun was coming up. The sky was pink and dotted with little clouds. The city glowed in front of them like it was made of gold. Nothing had ever looked so beautiful to George.

"It's . . . tomorrow," he said.

"No, it's today," Derrick corrected him. "Monday." He groaned. "Oh, man! We have school in a couple of hours."

"What time is it?" Renee asked.

George looked at his watch. "Five-thirty." His dad would be up in exactly one hour, the same time as every morning.

"Wow. We should all get home," Renee said.

"Yeah. George isn't the only one who should worry about getting in trouble. Even *my* parents would freak if they found out I was out all night," Shannon said.

Derrick shuddered. "I don't even want to *think* about what mine would do."

The three of them turned toward the street.

"Wait," George said.

They turned back, looking surprised.

"What about the treasure?" he asked.

Renee's eyebrows rose. "Treasure? George, there wasn't any treasure. Just an old book, remember?"

"I know, but don't you wonder what's in it?" George said. "I mean, what could be so important that Captain Kidd would go to all that trouble to hide it, and make a map, and all that?"

"Hey, you know, you have a point," Derrick said. His eyes lit up. "A very good point."

A grin spread across Shannon's face. "What are we waiting for?" she asked. Unzipping her jacket pocket, she pulled out the old book and handed it to George. "Start at the beginning."

Fifteen

A Pyrate's Oath

George turned the book over carefully in his hands. It wasn't much bigger than his father's pocket phone directory. The plain leather cover was dry, and bits of it flaked off on his fingers. All in all, it didn't look like much. But George got a funny feeling in his stomach when he thought of Captain Kidd hiding it all those hundreds of years before. What was that old saying? *You can't judge a book by its cover.*

He opened it to the first page and read,

The Last Testament of William Kidd

"Wow," he said. "It's for real. It was really his!"

"What's a testament?" Renee asked. "Like a diary or something?"

Shannon frowned. "A testament is a will, isn't it? Like when you leave your money to your heirs?"

"I like the sound of that," Derrick said. "Keep reading, George."

George turned to the next page. The writing was hard to read. It was in old-fashioned English, written with a quill pen. His eyes scanned the text, picking out a few words here and there. *I will a curse upon the one who did betraye me. . . . My best, and my best again to the worthy and brave. . . . I grant my love, Sarah . . . the four maps. . . . Beware misusing them, or ye shall invite doom. . . . The Eye of Eternity knows the true history. . . .*

"This is pretty weird stuff," he said. Making sense of Kidd's book was going to take a while. "It's like he wrote it in code."

But then George's eyes found a passage on the next page. He read out loud, "'My fortunate escape from death has made me cautious, so I have hidden my greatest treasure beneath my house.'"

"His greatest treasure!" Shannon said. "I hope he's not talking about this book."

"I don't think so. Check this out," George said. "'It is a treasure never meant to be mine. The Eye of Eternity is sought by greedy men, so great is its value. But the gem must be returned to its true owners.'"

"The gem? I *really* like the sound of that!" Derrick said.

"Me too!" Shannon said, laughing.

George's head was spinning. So there really was a treasure after all!

"Go on, go on," Derrick said. "Does he say where he hid it?"

George's eyes raced down the page. "'I have made maps to guide the worthy, but if any use them impetuously, they will find peril,'" he read. "'I have laid deadly traps, so that none unfit shall find it.'"

"Now, that I don't like so much," Derrick said. "More maps, more traps."

"Oh, we can handle them!" Shannon said with confidence.

"Totally," Renee agreed. "Especially now that we know a real treasure is down there!"

"What else does the book say?" Shannon asked. Everyone had forgotten about going home.

George turned the page and caught his breath. The page was titled:

Oaths of the Honorable Pyrate

"Wow, a real pirate oath!" he said.

Shannon peered over his shoulder. "Why does he spell *pirate* with a *y*?"

George shrugged. "It's just the old-time spelling. They used the letter *y* a lot more in Captain Kidd's time."

"I like it," said Renee. "I think we should take the oath, and then we'll be pyrates just like Captain Kidd—*pyrates* with a *y*!"

"I second that!" Derrick said.

George read out the oath to his three friends.

I. Be true and loyal to your captain.

II. Never steal from those who do not deserve it.

III. Spoils shall be shared justly.

IV. Never harm innocents.

"See?" George said. He felt triumphant. "Does that sound like someone who would cheat his partners and attack innocent ships? I always knew Captain Kidd was really a good guy."

"I like that oath," Shannon said. "No offense, George, but it's kind of, well, cooler than the one you made up. We should take it."

"Fine by me. Except for one thing," George said. "We don't have a captain."

Renee snorted.

"Yeah, whatever, George," said Shannon sarcastically.

"Are you kidding?" Derrick said.

They were all looking at George like he was crazy.

Renee put one hand on his shoulder. "George, *you're* our captain."

"Me?"

"Yeah. You planned the operations," Derrick said. "You made all the tough calls. And you talked Paul into trusting us."

"And you swore us to our first oath," Renee said.

George blinked. He had never felt like he was in charge. He'd just been doing what seemed to make sense. He'd wanted to find Kidd's treasure his whole life, had been studying pirates since he'd learned to read. Once he had found the map, everything had just sort of fallen into place, with a few narrow escapes from falling boulders and bad guys thrown in.

He felt his cheeks turning hot. "Well, if you're ready to take the oath and are up for another treasure hunt . . ."

"I am," said Renee. "I'm ready to be a pyrate."

"Me too," Derrick added.

George looked at Shannon. There was no doubt that she was braver than him. Stronger, too. She always wanted to go first. Maybe she also wanted . . .

She spat into her hand. "Let's swear on it, Captain George." She put her hand out in between them, palm up.

"Oh, great," Derrick said. "*Another* spit sandwich!"

The stakes get higher in Pyrates №2:
<u>*Eye of Eternity*</u>
Will George and his friends find the treasure—or will they meet their eternal end deep in Captain Kidd's mysterious tunnels?

"Now where?" George asked Paul. "Where'd you see the skeleton?"

"It's down this way," Paul replied. "But through a different tunnel."

He led them about twenty feet down the stream, then pointed out a small opening in the left wall.

"We have to be quiet now," Paul said. "Turn out the brights."

Once again they crawled into a small space in nearly complete darkness.

Then the tunnel turned.

Past the bend, there was not even a shred of light. George couldn't see a thing—not shapes, not outlines of the walls, not even his hand in front of his face. He breathed in nervously, with no idea what lay ahead of them. It was a strange feeling. He felt completely helpless.

"Can you see in here?" George asked Paul.

"No," Paul admitted. "Not now. But it's only a short tunnel."

Moving slowly, George and his friends shuffled along behind Paul.

"Do you know this tunnel well?" Shannon asked. George could hear the hesitancy in her voice.

Paul didn't answer for a few seconds. "I know it okay," he said finally. "I haven't been down here in a long time."

"But you're sure that it's short?" George asked. He tried to look around but saw nothing but blackness. "Paul, if you don't know where you're going, maybe I should be in front. I'm the captain."

"The what?"

George knew that his being captain meant nothing to Paul, but he still felt somehow responsible.

"I'm the—the leader, sort of. Trust me." George could hear that his friends had stopped, and he carefully felt his way ahead, passing Shannon, Derrick, Renee, and finally Paul. He put his arms out on either side, feeling the walls of the tunnel. Carefully, he stepped forward.

"All right, guys," he said, hoping he sounded more confident than he felt. "Let's go."

Slowly the five of them made their way farther down the tunnel. George could see that it wasn't getting any brighter—they weren't even close to the end. "Was the dead guy in this tunnel, Paul?"

he asked, feeling his way along the wall. "Or was he somewhere—"

Suddenly, he felt his toe smack into something hard in the floor. Without any warning, he pitched forward.

"Yahhh!"

Desperately, he used his arms to search the space in front of him for something to grab onto. But there was nothing. He couldn't see the walls of the tunnel, and he had no idea where he was falling. He flailed aimlessly, hoping to use his arms to catch himself when he fell.

"*Ahhh!*" George felt himself doubling over, about to land flat on his face on the rocky floor. His first thought was that this was going to be pretty painful. There was nothing to hold onto to slow himself down, and the ground in this tunnel was all uneven and sharp. And his second thought was that he was in bigger trouble than that.

Because there *wasn't* any ground in front of him. He went straight through the tunnel floor falling facefirst—into who knows what!